THE BILLIONAIRE'S UNEXPECTED ASSISTANT

Stephanie Guerrero

Copyright © Stephanie Guerrero 2019
Forget Me Not Romances, a division of Winged Publications

All rights reserved. No part of this publication may be reproduced, stored in a retrieval system, or transmitted in any form or by any means, with the exception of brief quotations in printed reviews.

This book is a work of fiction. The characters in this story are the product of the author's imagination and are completely fictitious.

All rights reserved.

ISBN: 9781708371074

"Jesus replied, 'I tell you the truth, if you have faith and do not doubt, not only can you do what was done to the fig tree, but also you can say to this mountain, "Go, throw yourself into the sea," and it will be done. If you believe, you will receive whatever you ask for in prayer'."
~Matthew 21:21-22

Chapter One

Jace Sheridan pulled up in front of a local FastTrip gas pump and dismounted his motorcycle to top off the tank. Swiping a bright yellow bandana from his back pocket, he blotted beads of sweat from his forehead and the back of his tan neck. *The autumn sun must be playing Indian summer*, he winced. Even his reflective aviator sunglasses couldn't keep back the glare of the afternoon sun.

When the pump registered a full tank, he hung up the nozzle. The afternoon ride called for a cold soda, candy bar and extra sunscreen. A blast of cold air washed over him as he stepped into a bright, clean, well ordered convenience store. The order surprised him, made him want to linger. He shook off the crazy sensation and headed for the candy bars.

Again, the dust free nature pleased him. Realization took root. Oil fires covered everything in soot and petroleum no matter how hard one tried to keep clean. Conscious of the grime covering his hands, he diverted to the men's room. The man staring back at him from the mirror could scare small children. Fire sunburn and oil residue covered his skin everywhere except the area usually covered by a bandana. His five o'clock needed grooming, and he needed a haircut.

Washing as best as the small bathroom allowed, he emerged a bit cleaner and more energized. Rapidly turning the corner, Jace slammed into lovely blonde carrying a flat of energy drinks. Metal cans clattered and spewed all over the floor, all over him and all over the surprised young woman. Feeling terrible, he bent to snag the spewing cans. He felt a gentle touch on his arm. The fresh-faced blonde smiled and beckoned to someone with her free hand.

"Don't worry about a thing. Carl here, is on clean up duty and will take care of it, won't you, Carl. Just head to the men's room and wash the sticky off." Her eyes lit like blue fire. "When you're clean, come to the front with your purchases, and April will make certain you are taken care of... on me."

He jerked a startled glance to her face. "But it is my fault, Ma'am. I'll take care of it," he stammered.

Again, she smiled. "It looks to me like you've been taking care of us... fighting the fires?"

He nodded, speechless.

"Then for once, let someone take care of you. We've got this." She grabbed a clean blue bandana from the end cap behind her and handed it to him. "Go on. Clean up. See you up front in a moment."

Five minutes and a clean bandana later, he

grabbed a peanut candy bar, orange soda, the strongest sunscreen the small store provided and headed to the counter. Determined to pay for his purchases and the spilled energy drinks, the blonde intercepted him. Pulling out her own wallet, she handed money to cover the accident to the cashier. It looked to be enough to cover his new bandana as well as his purchase.

Rare for a gas station convenience store, he mused. *Instead of having the store absorb the cost of his accident, the manager paid personally?* He opened his mouth to speak, but she silenced his protest with an outstretched hand.

"Lucy Christianson… once again, I apologize for getting you in such a sticky situation." She chuckled. "No pun intended. Again, I please accept my thanks for your work fighting the refinery fires."

Jace accept her slender hand and let her bright smile wash over him. Not one to waste time, he bowed over her hand and kissed it, "Ms. Christianson, apology accepted." She blushed. Aww… definitely a refreshing trait.

"Thank you, sir. If there is anything else, I can do for you, please let me know."

Still bent over her hand, he stood and looked her in the eye. "Actually… there is one thing, Ms. Christianson."

She pulled her hand from his grasp and took a step back at his forceful tone.

Too abrupt? He wondered. *Never…* "Come work for me," he proposed.

Blue eyes twinkled back at him. Is she laughing?

"Pardon me, Sir, but you never even gave me your name. Why on earth would I work for you?"

"Jace Sheridan," he answered with confidence.

The woman blinked. Didn't she know the name?

"I'm sorry, Sir. Is that supposed to mean something to me? If you'll excuse me." She waved the next customer forward in line and stepped toward the back office.

He followed, determined to finish the conversation. How could she not know him?

"Ms. Christianson, wait." He added a please. She turned, curious.

"Yes, Mr. Sheridan?"

"You truly don't who I am?"

"Should I?"

He stuck out his hand again, "Well, in that case, let me re-introduce myself... I am Jace Sheridan, owner of Sheridan Petroleum and Energy among other things. He allowed his arm to sweep the store. "Your people operate a well-oiled, clean, friendly, and honorable store here. Thanks to you if I'm not mistaken. You manage people well. I want you to come work for me."

Lucy tucked a piece of hair behind her ear and cocked her head in thought. He'd expected those blue eyes to glaze over, or to experience a bit of hero-worship awe. Instead, silence and calculating baby blues met him head on.

"The complement is unwarranted, Sir. A man of your caliber surely employs a number of people who jump at your beck and call. You don't know anything about me. What could you possibly want me to take care of?" She turned to go.

He raised an eyebrow, "Me."

Lucy took a step back and pulled out a can of Mace. Not the reaction he expected. He threw up both hands. "Hold on... I'm not a creep, but I am very badly in need of a personal manager. Someone to organize my world, make certain I remember meetings and have the proper names, deal with the details, if you will. As you can tell by my appearance today, I prefer getting my hands dirty than dealing with the corporate and society mess."

She put the Mace away. He was making headway. She checked her watch then pointed to his bike at the pump.

"Show me I.D."

He pulled out his wallet and displayed his name and face. She nodded toward the pump. "Ah... the cavalier billionaire. Your cycle is blocking the pump. I'll meet you outside. You can treat me to lunch and tell me all about your rash proposal."

Jace stood shocked. For the life of him, he could not remember the last time a woman held him at arm's length. The sensation oddly sparked his interest even further. Her words stung. Had she really called him 'the cavalier billionaire'? He shook off the sudden stupor and forced himself into action.

Stepping outside, he watched through the window as Miss Christianson entered the store office. After a brief moment, she exited the building. With long-legged graceful strides, she approached him.

"Are you okay with seafood?" Her suggestion

brought relief. After making decisions all day every day, initiation pleased him. His mouth began to salivate. He loved seafood, but decided to play it cool having already made buffoon of himself more than once. First dumping sticky drinks on the lovely manager, then asking her to take care of him... yeah, not his best moves.

Thumbs up, he nodded. "Absolutely, seafood is great. Lead the way, ma'am," he added with a slight bow. She raised an eyebrow at his fumbled attempt at chivalry. Was he that rusty? Society women laughed at his jokes, often swooned if he offered them anything, yet *this* woman

appeared unimpressed.

Straddling his bike, he turned the ignition and headed out after her small, purple two door coup. The car screamed order for a middle of the road model. Clean down to the hub caps, not a bit of clutter showed when she opened the door. Little touches revealed the personality of the owner. A custom leather steering wheel cover and floor mats, a fragrance in the shape of a tropic flower on the rearview mirror and the color of the car... purple suggested the same combination of order and joyful spirit he detected earlier.

He chuckled at his analysis using a car. Yep, his love of cars definitely showed. Jace followed her into a tiny parking lot adjacent to an old shanty by the water. Interesting, unassuming... he never would have noticed the place.

Lucy stepped from her car with a grin and raised eyebrow. "I hope you like fresh... they pull them out of the water and serve them up here. Pops puts all the love into the food and only enough into the building to keep it up to code.

He grinned back at her test of his character. As long as the food satisfied, he didn't care what the building looked like.

"Bring it on, sounds amazing, Lucy. Thanks." Her eyes narrowed at his use of her first name. Nodding, she turned, expecting him to follow.

Lucy forced her feet to move toward Pop's Seafood Shanty, a local haunt. When Jace Sheridan pulled up in front of the FastTrip, she never realized the identity of the man. When he'd bumped into her, she'd done her best not to stare. His face looked familiar. Not until he flashed the I.D. did realization smack her in the face. She knew of the man... all too well. If her family knew of the man's sudden proposal, she wouldn't have a moment's peace.

When he made the assumption that she managed the place and asked her to take care of him... knock her over with a feather. In some way, the Fast Stop owed its pristine order to her care since the owner hired whomever she sent his way, and she checked up on her people regularly, she mused.

Most women would delight to hear one of the world's wealthiest, most eligible bachelors say those words, but... she needed more. Rather than snag a billionaire, she preferred to find a love worth a billion dollars, but for her family's sake, she would hear out his crazy proposal about hiring her as a personal assistant.

Opening the door of her favorite purchase, she

slipped into her pristine auto and inhaled the smell of leather. Somehow, this little car always relaxed her. The offer of personal assistant hit her full force as she pulled into traffic and checked the rearview mirror to see if her billionaire "boss" followed behind.

She understood the job of personal assistant to the rich and powerful. Being at the beck and call of an individual, making the impossible become possible required devotion. Could she find devotion toward a man who filled such an important decision on a whim? Memory of their brief encounter in the gas station flashed back into her brain. He'd been polite, not egotistical at all, just… spontaneous not the vibe she received from the papers or other community sources. Typically, his interviews displayed confidence.

Right then and there, she'd felt a nudge to play it cool. She would never lie, yet caution demanded she reserve judgment and not fawn over the man like every other female. So, now what should she do with him? Should she really consider his crazy offer? She sent a prayer heavenward.

Pointing toward a seaside table, she hoped the handsome billionaire would take a seat while she took just one more moment. When she returned from reapplying her makeup in the ladies' room, Sheridan stood and held out her chair.

"I ordered the appetizer sampler." He nodded toward the platter in the center of the table. "I didn't know your drink preference, so I just asked for water with lemon. Have a seat."

His tone demanded obedience. Years cultivating

independence resisted, but again, she felt a quiet whisper to yield in kindness to the man across from her.

"Thank you. I appreciate the thoughtfulness." Lucy chose her calm response and folded her shaky hands in her lap where they couldn't be seen. "Now tell me. How may I assist you, Mr. Sheridan?"

The tanned, well-muscled man across from her crossed his arms. The corners of his mouth lifted in an apologetic grin. "Not my best moment back there in the store, I'll admit." He rubbed his jaw. "I've been up since two am this morning in the midst of smoke and fire. Your calm in the midst of chaos welcomed me in a way I haven't experienced in a long time."

He extended a hand toward her across the table. "Let's start over. I'm Jace Sheridan, owner and president of Sheridan Energy. I'd like to talk with you about a job opening that recently opened up, Ms. Christianson."

She accepted the handshake never expecting the tingling sensation that shot through her body. A quick release seemed the best option. Keeping a straight face, she reclaimed her seat and reached for her appetizer plate.

"I'm listening, but I'll admit, I'm not certain I want to accept what you're offering. I've developed a life I enjoy." She snagged a crab cake and picked up her fork.

Jace nodded, leaned forward and grabbed a crab cake of his own. The sound of the ocean waves washing gently against the pier mixed with the cry of the seagulls. She managed a deep cleansing breath. The feeling that change loomed just around the corner settled.

God, whatever is coming... is it Your plan for me? I really need peace right now.

Your job is to bring peace into his world.

Lucy stared at the gorgeous man across from her with new eyes. Bring peace to his world...?

"What you're looking for is peace, Mr. Sheridan, order brought to chaos...?"

His deep brown eyes widened. She must have hit the mark.

Thank you, Lord.

"That is exactly what I need, Ms. Christianson! My father's administrative assistant served as my own until her retirement last fall. I've been too busy to search through a bunch of applicants, so a number of secretaries and assistants to other board members have been filling in the gap."

Lucy shook her head. "Sounds a bit chaotic without a central point of contact to the boss."

Jace leaned back in his chair. *How can I already be thinking of him as Jace?*

"You have no idea. Duplicate memos, misplaced fundraiser gala tickets, three separate ladies told I would escort them to the same society function, clients incorrectly informed of meetings... the list goes on. To be honest, fighting the oil fires proved less complicated this week than handling my schedule."

Lucy motioned for the waiter. "Do you mind if I order the daily special for both of us? You won't regret it?"

A contented sigh actually escaped the man's

lips. "Having someone else make a decision on something would be fabulous. Order away, Ms. Christianson, or may I call you Lucy?"

She ordered two seafood platters and a couple of Arnold Palmers. The half lemonade, half tea drink refreshed the soul. She sat back in her chair and studied the well-known man across from her. Jace Sheridan, billionaire extraordinaire moved constantly. Bouncing a knee, tapping a toe, drumming his fingers on the red and white tablecloth created a feeling of electricity around him.

Confident movement, excitement to be on to the subsequent adventure oozed from his mannerisms. Even in their brief meeting, she sensed his desire to settle the matter and be on the next plane.

What loose ends must he leave in his wake, she wondered? If her impressions proved true, the man's genius needed to be harnessed and handled well. He truly required a keeper.

"Are you married, Ms. Christianson, or in a relationship?" His sudden interjection into her thoughts startled her.

She blanched. "I don't see how that is any of your business, MR. Sheridan." Suddenly, the conversation felt very uncomfortable.

He held up a hand meant to stop her mental train from running away. "Nothing personal, I maintain a very demanding schedule. I'm on call twenty-four hours a day. My assistant would be the same. I own a very large estate in Georgia with a fully furnished guest home for just such a person. If you have a family or a serious relationship, this job would be too demanding. I provide a large income in exchange for a high demand on your time."

He wrote a six figured number on a napkin and turned it her direction.

"At that salary, you must be very demanding." The sarcastic remark slipped off her lips for lack of a better response.

"I am." His tone reverted to all business, and his eyes bored into hers.

The steaming seafood platters appeared interrupting the conversation. Jace exclaimed over the food. She asked several more questions.

He answered patiently then leaned forward, raised one handsome dark eyebrow and made one non-negotiable demand…

"Miss Christianson, should you accept, I require that you pack light, leave immediately and start at once. Anything you need, I will provide in route. Any lose ends that need tying, you can tie as we go. Such is my life… always on the go."

She crossed her arms and cocked her head to study the reckless, commanding alpha. What could possibly be drawing her to comply? The outrageous salary he offered definitely matched his equally outrageous demands. The generous offer might tantalize many, but money never motivated her. She steepled her fingers and touched them to her lips in thought. The move caused the man's eyes to widen. Did he think she would leap without thinking the idea through?

She shook her head at the spinning series of events. Other than the Fast Trip workers, there were no real goodbyes to be made. Her closest family consisted of an auntie in Maine and a cousin in Europe. Her cat, Pumpkin, would learn to travel. Her heart tugged her toward the magnetic man, yet it wasn't his magnetism drawing her in. He needed her, and from the moment he asked for help, her heart answered. For reasons beyond her understanding, she chose to accept.

"For reasons, I'm speechless to express, I accept your offer. I simply feel called to bring peace to your world. I'll have a friend drop me at your offices by five o'clock, Mr. Sheridan, unless there is somewhere else you prefer?"

He leaned back and grinned. "The Butterfield airport, ten miles south of the city will do." Standing, he leaned across the table and shook her hand. "I'll settle up with the waiter and let you get a head start. Welcome to the chaos of my world, Miss Christianson." His dark eyebrows lifted as he nodded his head in a gallant salute.

One corner of her lips lifted in a smile, parting slightly. "No, Mr. Sheridan… welcome to the calm that is mine." She started toward the exit, but paused to glance over her shoulder. The man stared after her with his mouth agape. "See you at the airport. Get the engines running. I won't be late."

After making a decision, Jace rarely looked back, but something about today's decision left him sweating bullets. Had it been reckless? Most would say so. Hiring a stranger without a background check to run your billion-dollar life on a whim appeared wildly irresponsible. He'd learned to trust his gut, and his instincts insisted he hire the calm, unruffled woman from the convenience store. From his clumsy accident to his wild proposal, she remained composed, kind and efficient. He believed actions revealed character.

He checked his watch and signaled to the pilot to start the engines. Would Lucy Christianson be true to her word? At twenty minutes until five, he paced the tarmac until spotting the little purple car turn up the drive. He checked his watch. Fifteen minutes early with only two large suitcases and a pet carrier. Not bad...

Jace made short work of the distance to her car as she hugged what appeared to be the store clerk named April. He nodded at the young woman and grabbed Lucy's bags.

"I'm eternally grateful, Lucy. Ready for a grand adventure?" he grinned.

Her adventurous smile shot straight to his heart.

"I believe we've got a plane to catch," she shouted against the noise of the engines. "Let's go."

Chapter Two

The four hour flight home dragged into eight days as his disorganized staff continued to divert his flights to various problematic locations needing the firm hand of the boss. Since his father's death and the last assistant's retirement, his company and the family interests swirled in never-ending chaos. Even his overactive brain and metabolism felt the strain.

What an introduction to the whirlwind, he muttered.

Jace stared at the willowy, slumped form of his new personal assistant. Throughout the chaotic flight schedule, Lucy remained a beacon. Now, even in sleep, she exuded peace. Odd really, that a woman so well-ordered and peaceful would agree to leave her known world for his unknown. She stepped away from the safe for the uncertain and let the storm rage around her.

Sure, he knew there were perks to working for a wealthy, eligible bachelor, but he excelled at reading the signs of the greedy and power-hungry. She seemed genuinely interested in bringing order to his world. The thought refreshed him.

As usual, sleep evaded him. Details swirled in his over active brain. His personal sports car would be waiting for them at the private airport. He dialed his housekeeper to make sure arrangements for the guest house were ready. For the first time in months, excitement filled him at the prospect of heading home.

Lucy Christianson... He pulled out his phone and looked up the meaning and origin of her name, an odd hobby he enjoyed. Delight brightened his brain.

Hmmm... Lucy means light. How ironic since my last name, Sheridan, also means light. She certainly brightened my world the moment she walked into it. The thought settled.

Did he bring light to others? He tried. Magazines and paparazzi looked for the flashy light of his life. The fast cars, a different woman at every event seemed expected. Sometimes he gave them what they were looking for, but the persona he presented to the world wasn't the real Jace Sheridan. Lucy felt real. Time would tell. In his world, real didn't last.

The plane touched down on the tarmac, and Lucy blinked. He grinned. He assumed her age to be in the late twenties. In hiring her on instinct, he had not stopped to find out. Tall, golden brown hair, tan with an athletic figure evident in her simple slacks and salmon blouse; she exuded a wholesome beauty, not the exotic model type who normally surrounded him. Still, she offered him what the others could not... order in his chaotic world. Something about her just radiated peace.

She rubbed a hand across her hazel green-brown eyes. "How long did I sleep?" she whispered sheepishly.

"A few hours. This leg is over. We're finally home." He couldn't keep the excitement from his voice. In the evening sun, his white-columned, Southern-style estate glistened. Hollywood A-listers, politicians, foreign dignitaries and sports stars clamored for invites the few times of year he allowed his home open to entertain, but tonight felt different. The elaborate guest house belonged to Lucy now, and like a kid giving a gift on Christmas, he couldn't wait to show his new assistant the perks in working for him.

A moment later, the plane came to a stop, and the pilot opened the door. They exited the plane, heading directly for Jace's car. The shiny, black, sports car with red leather interior beckoned.

"Lucy, meet my best girl, Ebony."

"You *name* your cars?" Lucy flashed a teasing smile.

"Hey, this girl and I spend a lot of quality time together. I restored her myself. Lesson number one... never knock a man's car. It's the same as knocking a man's ego." He put her luggage in the trunk and opened the door for her. He nodded toward the pet carrier.

"Poor cat. You've dragged it all over this nation. I never would have pegged you as a cat lover. You don't strike me as the type to want a shedding mess," he winced at the orange and white furball in the small pet carrier.

Lucy's eyes twinkled. "Pumpkin is my best friend. Never knock a girl's cat. When you can't find a great guy, a cat is the next best thing."

He shut her door and jogging around to the driver's side, slid into the car. "Really…? A cat is the next best thing to a man in your life? I don't see it."

Lucy clutched the carrier close. "They take care of themselves, love to snuggle and are extremely loyal."

He shot her a skeptical sideways glance as he started the car. "If you say so, Ms. Christianson. Hold on tight. Pumpkin is about to get a taste of life in the fast lane."

Jace took perverse pleasure in driving a bit faster than normal, that is until he glanced at Pumpkin and saw the terror in the cat's widened eyes. Lucy's eyes, however, sparkled, revealing an adventurous heart. He eased back on the throttle feeling both guilty for messing with the cat and confused with the woman he hired. A calm, organized, adrenaline junkie…? Be still his beating heart. He shoved the traitorous organ down and placed it under lock and key.

"Apologize to Pumpkin for me. Sometimes Ebony and I get a bit caught up in the moment. Your cat is not impressed."

Lucy laughed. "Pumpkin lives at his own pace. This is a bit fast for him"

Jace shot her an inquisitive look. "But not too fast for you?" he questioned.

"I confess, I have a weakness for anything fast,

and I haven't indulged the need for speed since the skydiving incident. No..." she paused with a slender finger on her pursed lips. "Actually, since this spring at the Daytona 500 when Sam let me drive his..." she stopped when she noticed his jaw dropped to the floor. "Sorry for rambling. Anyway, this is a real treat. Thank you."

"Lucy Christianson, there is more to you than meets the eye! Remind me to ask about the skydiving incident." He tucked the knowledge of her adventures into a back corner of his brain as the car pulled up the long drive and stopped in front of the estate.

He expected Lucy to gawk and fawn over the massive estate, but once again, she surprised him. She paid more attention to her terrified furball than his million-dollar mansion. An unfamiliar sensation stirred for the second time in one day.

Stepping out of the sports car, he tossed the keys to his household manager and nodded to the back of the car. A domestic assistant ran to the back and tugged Lucy's luggage from the trunk as a familiar redhead stepped out of the house. The woman visibly winced at the combination of Lucy, her cat and her bags.

He shook his head. "Now, Mandy, don't go jumping to conclusions. Allow me to introduce my new administrative assistant, Lucy Christianson. I hired her to fill the gap Beverly left. The guest house is her home now, so no more using it to avoid me on weekends," he winked and gave the teenager a hug.

"Lucy, meet my annoying half-sister, Miranda.

She just enrolled for her next college semester. Now, it's late, let me show you to the guest house.

Jenkins, the household manager walked up and interrupted. "Pardon me, Sir… but you are expected at the Wildlife Preservation Gala in an hour. I have your tuxedo laid out in your quarters. Need I remind you, that you are the face of the Energy sector, Sir?

Jace slapped his forehead. In the chaos of the past few days, he'd forgotten the event. Inspiration struck. He glanced over at his sister and Miss Christianson.

"Jenkins, thank you for the reminder, but forget the tuxedo. These jeans, boots and a colorful shirt will do. It makes me approachable. Miss Christianson, I know its abrupt, but again, such is my life. You'll attend with me this evening. I'll introduce you around, let people get to know you as the face when I'm not around. You may go as you are, just…"

"Sis, drum up some sort of pearls or something for Lucy and then head off to finish your homework, will ya?" Miranda made a face at him and then linked arms with a wide-eyed Lucy. Aww, so the unflappable Miss Christianson could be rattled. The thought somehow pleased him.

"Miss Christianson, be ready in half an hour…" he turned to go, but she stopped him in his tracks.

"Mr. Sheridan, a moment…"

"Yes."

"The role you just described is that of a plus one, not a personal assistant. I need to understand the parameters of this job if I'm to help."

He thought for a brief moment. "Your job is to

be anything I require. Escorting a different super model or actress to each event is exhausting. I need someone to work the room with me... to get a feel for the community or clients without my explaining every impression."

She stifled a gasp, but he heard it. "Is there a problem, Miss Christianson."

She straightened leaving him to believe he imagined her reaction. "I am fully capable of meeting those requirements, Mr. Sheridan. I have only one request. I can work a room, but I will not do reporter interviews. It's not negotiable."

The demand startled him. Not many would issue a demand and walk away from a six-figure job. Interviews were a small price to pay if Miss Christianson could organize his world. He nodded agreement, but as he stepped into the next room he paused when he heard his new assistant's voice. The woman intrigued him. He needed more information. He listened as she spoke to his half-sister sister.

"Does your brother ever stop to breathe?" she whispered.

"Never," Miranda rolled her eyes and grinned. "but the good news... I get to go back to college next week. You... get make sure Jace gets his head out of the stratosphere and into the world where the normal people function. I definitely get the better end of the deal.

Heads up? He's supposed to fly to Geneva next week for a World Energy Summit. You'll need to make sure you are both well informed, well dressed and well spoken... and he probably won't tell you about it until the day before." The college student winked. "Thought I'd give you a running start, since all those before you failed miserably."

"Why?"

Miranda raised an eyebrow. "Because my brother is brilliant, distracted and keeps all the details filed away in that great brain of his instead of on paper. The others just couldn't keep up. Think A.D.D. mixed with a true genius. Add to that, the chaos and change created by our father's death and catering to his maternal grandfather's demands for help in the old country, and you are entering the whirlwind.

To work for my brother, you can't wait for orders, you have to anticipate needs and control the chaos, so he doesn't have to. He needs someone who can handle the everyday details of his complicated life and allow him to be brilliant."

"Why give me a heads up?"

"Because for the first time, Jenkins' reminder of an event didn't throw him into a grumpy state, and you handled his demands with grace. To continue to do so without warning is exhausting unless you know to anticipate it. I want my brother to find peace and relief before I head back to school. I'm hoping you're the answer."

Jace leaned back against the wall and sent up a prayer for the first time in a long time. Peace nestled in Miss Christianson's blue eyes. The calm she brought just walking into a room soothed his weary heart and brought hope to his soul.

The moment Jace Christianson and his sister

parted ways, Jenkins showed Lucy to her guest house. The two-story white brick columned home graced the entrance to lush gardens and an Olympic size pool offering a lovely respite to those with the time to use it. Tonight, instead of a lovely swim, she needed information.

From first-hand experience, she knew knowledge meant power. The best personal assistants stayed ahead of the curve and knowledge provided that insight.

"Jenkins," she turned to the stately gentleman. "Would you have access to a guest list at the venue tonight? If I'm to help work a room, it's helpful to know who's attending."

The man beamed. "I'll have the information for you by the time you're at the curb, Miss. Welcome aboard. It's good to have someone looking out for Mr. Sheridan again."

"Let me give you my number, so we may communicate in the future. If possible, could you text or email the list to me?"

He bowed slightly. "Consider it done."

After a quick shower, and a change into fitted jeans, an ice blue silk blouse, and heels, Lucy paused by the pool and opened her Bible App. Taking time to reconnect with her Lord mattered. *Lord, You are the air I breathe. Thank you for the opportunity to shine your light tonight. I trust you to provide all I need.*

She settled on Philippians 4:9, "The things you have learned and receive and heard and seen in me, practice these things; and the God of peace shall be with you." The verse filled her lungs with fresh peace.

Jenkins texted the list. She forwarded it to her contacts with a smile. The God of all grace supplied her with the tools to complete this mission. For whatever reason, Jace Sheridan needed His touch. She headed for the front of the house. Jace sat waiting in a McLaren P-14 convertible. The glossy paint shimmered from reds, to orange to golds giving the impression the low-riding sports car lit the road in a streak of flames. She grinned.

Speed... ahh... life. His choice in vehicles sparked her excitement. Tonight, unbeknownst to her boss, the two of them would set the world on fire. He nodded his admiration at her choice of attire and waited as the valet opened her door. Armed with her secret arsenal of information, she craved speed. Lowering her sunglasses, she tapped the dash and turned to her new boss.

"Is there an open road where we can cut this baby loose?"

Jace Sheridan's ever-present grin widened until his attractive dimples clearly displayed. "A stretch along my private beachfront property... it's a bit longer, but I think we can make up the time if you're game, Miss Christianson?"

"Bring it, boss."

The revving engine sang. The wind ripped through her hair, but the look on Jace's face and her own combined their shared joy. They arrived on time. She slipped a comb into his hand and tugged a brush out of her purse for a quick touch up as he slowed.

Jace tossed the keys to the valet, and crossed in

front of the car to open her door. She took his offered hand.

"Miss Christianson, you are a joy to drive," he tipped his head to her.

She quirked a smile and raised one eyebrow as she stepped inside the lovely beach mansion. "You should see me behind the wheel," she winked. Her boss grinned and offered his arm.

Love at first sight is for fairy-tales, Jace repeated for the fifth time since the fast ride to the Fundraiser. *Besides, you know the rules.* Frustration threatened to surface. Finding an eligible mate, who loved what he loved, *and* garnered the approval of his powerful family felt impossible, but tonight, watching Miss Christianson greet influential people by name and ask after their children or hobbies equated to studying a master artist at work. How did she manage?

Several times, she pulled him aside and whispered a momentous tidbit of information in his ear making him look competent and prepared. Now, exhaustion crinkled at the corners of her eyes and her sparkle dimmed. Time to rescue his lovely miracle worker…

He stepped up to an elderly gentleman who held Lucy captive, and nodded with a smile. "Forgive me, Senator. I fear I must take this lovely lady and whisk her away."

The gentleman's disappointment showed, but so did Lucy's relief.

He said goodnight for them both and called for the car. Five minutes down the road, she let her eyes flutter closed. He hated to wake her, but he had to know...

"Miss Christianson... how did you manage to take the room by storm tonight?"

She yawned. "Knowledge is power, Mr. Sheridan, as you are aware. Krister retrieved a copy of the guest list as I got dressed this evening. I used certain resources to look up pictures, names and details of key players in the interest of your company and personal influence and had it all sent to my phone. The rest is easy. Glad I could be of assistance. I *love* your car..." her voice waned as sleep beckoned. He let her rest.

What resources? He wondered. Whatever they were, gratitude welled up in his heart. The woman asleep in his car already proved worth her weight in gold. Instead of drained, he felt energized and couldn't wait for a new day.

Music rang out in the dark bedroom. Lucy groaned and rolled over, shoving off the plush down comforter and scrambling for her phone. *Four-thirty in the morning...? Who could be calling at this hour?*

Rubbing her eyes, she picked up the phone and answered in a groggy voice. Jace Sheridan began talking a mile a minute. She blinked and turned on the lamp before telling him to start over.

"Miss Christianson, get the plane ready to fly, and let me know how soon we can leave! I'm on the other line with my Israel natural gas partners. Due to a missile attack, we have a containment problem that requires out of the box thinking. I'm trying to help via video conference, but we need to be there stat!"

He hung up the phone, leaving her groggy mind to process it all. She dialed him back.

"Yes?" He snapped impatiently.

"Link our phones, so that I have your contact list, and I will get the plane ready."

He sounded relieved. A moment of silence passed. "Done."

"Consider the plane ready to fly. I'll let you know when we are wheels up."

The contacts arrived a moment later. The sleepy pilot promised to get to the airport immediately, and have a plane ready in an hour. She texted the boss to meet her at the door in twenty minutes.

Grateful her clothes still rested packed in her suitcases; she took time for a hot shower.

At this rate, she mused, *I might as well leave them packed and keep a bag aboard the plane for emergencies.* A designer jogging suit, a bit of lip gloss and her blonde tangles up in a messy ponytail, helped her feel almost human. She ran a hand over her face and took a deep breath before grabbing her suitcases. No use waking the staff unless absolutely necessary.

A soft tap on the guest house door surprised her. Jace Sheridan handed her a latte and motioned for a young man to take her bags.

"Peace offering accepted..." she mumbled over the foam.

He managed a faint smile. "Good to know. Hop in. You said the pilot will be ready for us?" The skepticism bounced off her tired mind.

"Ready, waiting and with breakfast of some

sort. Said he can't fly at night without sustenance so I told him to triple the order."

He merely nodded and sped the roadster down the road. *In for a penny, in for a pound...* she mused. Jace accepted a hands-free call and began to trouble shoot. His brilliant ability to diagnose a problem sight unseen and come up with unique solution became more evident as the call continued. She wondered at her role once they boarded the flight.

Jace parked the sports car inside a private hanger and nearly ran to the plane leaving her to fend for herself. The pilot stepped forward to help as she struggled with her bags.

"Welcome to Team Sheridan..." The man had the audacity to grin.

Chapter Three

Exhausted didn't begin to describe Lucy's mental state. The job of personal assistant was one she would never take for granted again. Jace's brain never stopped, and he expected those around him to understand his incomplete sentences, to fill in the gaps and to anticipate. Right now, knee deep in Israeli natural gas refineries and oil drilling specs his need for her dwindled. He gave her leave to catch up on rest, but who could sleep with so many glorious sights to see?

Calling ahead to the Ron Beach Hotel in Tiberias, she secured a room overlooking the peaceful Sea of Galilee and chartered a small wooden fishing boat to take her out on the water. The fisherman hesitated and glanced at the sky. She tripled his posted price and asked for a few minutes on the water. The man agreed.

The sunset shimmered on the calm waters turning the sloping hillsides a dusty rose. She took a slow, deep breath and imagined her Lord on the hillside across the waters teaching the Sermon on the Mount.

This place reminds me of the calm my Savior brings to every storm, she reflected. Just like a number of storms Christ calmed upon the very seas in front of her. The wind whipped through her hair. She wrapped her jacket tighter and glanced at her guide. The man pointed to a few small clouds just visible on the horizon.

"We must make for shore, Miss. These winter storms whip up out of nowhere. I've seen the waves reach twelve feet. At merely five feet, I struggle to dock the boat. The wind is picking up."

She nodded and hunkered down as he pointed the boat toward land.

"Calm in the storm…" she whispered. "Peace on the battlefield… Father, renew my spirit and flood through me, so that I may offer hope and peace to those around me," she prayed.

Once settled back in the lovely hotel, she savored the bountiful buffet of fresh dates, avocados, salads and fruits of every variety along with numerous entrees. The storm raged around them, but the peaceful atmosphere in the pleasant rooms filled her soul. The small break in her hectic role as personal assistant reminded her to trust God to calm the turmoil around her, and not rely on her power, strength, intelligence or resources.

Morning dawned with fresh purpose and a call that Jace needed her on board the plane in two hours. She planned a return trip. So many places needed exploring: Nazareth, Megiddo, Mt. Carmel, and so many more. Honeycomb, blintzes, fresh fruit and fish offered the perfect morning start to prepare her for Jace's next adventure.

"Calm in the storm… Father. Thank you for being my calm in the storm."

An hour and a half later, she arrived at the plane feeling refreshed. Jace glanced up from his phone and his frown turned into a wide smile. He reached a hand and brushed the hair from her face surprising them both. He cleared his throat and pulled back.

"You seem refreshed. Ready for the next adventure? Duty calls. The office staff are clamoring to meet my new personal assistant. We'll arrive just before midnight Eastern time, so make certain to get a good night's sleep. I've called a meeting after we get back to introduce you to the staff. Good work at handling my details, Miss Christianson. I hope you got a bit of rest. I've learned to grab it while I can."

Upon arriving at home, Jace's memo demanded all senior staff and administrative help meet in the board room. All personnel attended promptly… with the exception of Jace himself. The man was MIA.

Somehow, Lucy needed to get ahead of him before the World Energy Summit. With no one to take point, the fractured state of his office staff created chaos … until now. She wondered if she'd taken on too great a project. Looking around the conference table, she assessed the willing, tired faces and took charge. Only one individual, the company VP, stood against the wall with arms crossed and brow furrowed as if evaluating whether or not she posed a threat. Well, she wasn't hired to run the company. Her job existed to keep the boss organized and supplied with information and well-maintained schedules.

"Good morning!" she smiled. Thank you all for attending so promptly. Mister Sheridan called you together in order to introduce me as his new personal assistant. I'm not here to run the company or your lives, but *everything* needing Mr. Sheridan's attention comes through me from now on.

With that being said, I'd like to hear each of you introduce yourself, state your departments and have a brief outline on the best way to streamline your communications with me. Information is power, and power is what Sheridan Energy and Technology does best.

I will be traveling with Mr. Sheridan, so you may contact me through email or funnel your requests through my assistant April." She smiled at the former Fast Trip employee. Having someone reliable and familiar provided a solid foundation, and she definitely needed to find her footing.

Thirty minutes later, a round of applause and visible sighs of relief met her ears. Even the disgruntled VP seemed on board. She spent the rest of the day streamlining the office structure, answering memos, syncing the boss' schedule to a central server, canceling models lined out to attend events and finally falling asleep at her desk. April called a limo to take her home.

The crystal waters of her pool beckoned. Slipping into a modest silver swimsuit, she began swimming laps. The heated waters soothed her soul. A splash entered the deep end as she came up for air. She froze. Who else had access?

Her boss' head poked out of the water so close their noses nearly touched. Jace shook his head and rubbed the water from his face in shock. Her pulse raced at his nearness.

"Lucy?" His dark eyes scanned her briefly in surprise. He blinked. "Oh man. It's been so long since anyone used the pool. My father's old assistant never came in… Not once did I think..." His words faded off, and he put a discreet distance between them.

"Would you like me to leave?" He offered.

She ran her hand over her face and hair. "You need the refreshment as well. I'll leave." She made a move to exit, when he touched her arm. Her skin tingled at his touch. His eyes shot to hers, and he let go.

"Please. Surely, we can share the water. I'm just here to swim a few laps. With our crazy schedules, I grab the exercise when I can. It appears you had the same thought. Stay. I'll take the left?"

Lucy relaxed. "Last one to complete thirty laps buys pizza?" She shocked herself with the offer. What about this man allowed her to be herself?"

He grinned at her suggestion and made his way to the end of the pool. "Best offer I've had all day! I've been up to my ears dealing with the family holdings. You're on!"

Thirty laps later, Jace tapped the side first. Five seconds behind him, she tapped the concrete and caught her breath. It felt good. A gentleman, he climbed out first and tossed her a white, Egyptian cotton towel. She patted her face and stepped out, wrapping the towel modestly around her.

"I'm buying, boss. What do you like?" She grinned.

"Pepperoni, what else is there?" He teased and dangled the keys to his car. "If you order, I'll let you drive. How long does it take you to change?"

She clapped her hands in glee. "Twenty minutes?"

"Deal. You call in the pizza. I'll call for the car. It's a great night for a drive, agreed?"

Her lips curved in a grin.

"Despite being absent for the meeting today... you're alright, Boss," she teased. "But I do have an early morning at the office, so no late night for this girl."

His eyes met hers in understanding. He nodded. "Or for this guy either. With the Geneva Summit coming up, we need all the rest we can get. He checked his phone for the time.

"Pizza, a quick drive, and I drop you off by ten ?" She nodded and ran to change.

The evening swim, pizza, quick drive and an actual good night sleep refreshed her body, mind and spirit... until an hour into work the next morning when her cell phone rang. The roar of jet engines echoed through the phone when she answered.

"Lucy... Where are you? We are wheels up in twenty minutes!" Jace shouted through the noise.

"Where am I? Where are you? You called another company staff meeting, remember?" She couldn't keep the tinge of frustration from seeping through her voice.

"Ah… that's right. I trust you handled it. Now… I need you here."

"Mr. Sheridan, there are a number of things that need attention…"

"… and all of them can be handled by phone or through that new lovely assistant you brought on today, Amanda, right?"

"April! She's only been on the job for two hours! Where are we headed, Mr. Sheridan?"

"Really, Lucy," he shouted. "I thought I asked you to call me Jace. Anyway, the President called, and on our way to the Geneva Summit, he needs us to swing by Poland. In addition to that, I'll be presenting the council on what, if any, effects human energy production has on the climate. Jenkins packed for you, and I sent the car. It should be outside waiting. See you in a few. Oh, the President's daughter will be flying with us, along with a reporter and a friend of mine from college." The phone clicked.

Lucy plopped into her new comfortable office chair and swiveled to stare out the glass window as Jace's personal limo pulled up to the front door. Words failed her. She hung up the phone, leisurely finished the rest of her soda and took a moment to breath. They could wait an extra few minutes for her to clear her head and make certain April and a few others were aware of the new itinerary.

She buzzed her assistant, and a moment later, April arrived tablet in hand. Lucy leaned forward in her chair and steepled her hands in thought.

"April, Mr. Sheridan called, and I'm needed out of town a day earlier, starting immediately, so take a list of items down and get the information to me as soon as possible. I need to know the following:

*How long is the Geneva Summit?

*Are there any other major energy or tech forums happening in the not so distant future? Have we received invitations to anything lately? If so, I need them all forwarded to my personal device immediately." She shook her head. "I've got to get ahead of the curve."

*"I need all company data or reports compiled in a readable presentation with charts on any environmental impact, good or bad, that we as a company have directly or indirectly caused, experienced or researched AND, I need it in the next eight, no… ten hours.

*Lastly, I need gala wear in these sizes delivered to the Geneva airport by the time we arrive from some local shop. I prefer ice blue, but whatever you can find will do. I have a feeling I'm going to be dragged to these events, and I need to be prepared."

Placing a hand to her throbbing head, she glanced up in time to see April's quirky grin. In times past, they'd been a great team. Calling her in added stability to the whirlwind. Lucy could manage Jace, and April would catch the loose ends. Teamwork.

"April, how am I doing? I'm meeting myself coming and going. I feel like I'm on a ride that spins in circles and doesn't stop! Does it show?"

April leaned against the mahogany desk and shook her head. "To the company heads, you are a hero. They have no idea the boss didn't show this morning, although some might suspect it. The overall attitude is a huge sigh of relief to have someone to contact and funnel needs through."

She checked her clipboard. "I just sent a memo requiring detailed reports and any requests from each sector by Friday, with an addendum that they will receive a reply in two weeks. I'll forward their reports as they come in. The response is positive. Breathe, Boss. You've got this. I've got your back. Now… your car is waiting. I'll keep things stable on this end. Enjoy your trip."

Inside the car, Lucy leaned her head back against the headrest and shut her eyes against the whirlwind. The earthy smell of coffee tantalized her nostrils. The limo driver, she couldn't place his name… handed her a mocha with extra whipped cream.

"Oh my…You are a life-saver! I'm sorry, I've already forgotten your name, but I'll get better. I'm meeting myself coming and going."

The old driver grinned into the rearview mirror and tipped his cap. "No worries, Miss. It's Carl. Take the time on the way to the airport to catch up to yourself," he winked. "If its any consolation, you've lasted longer than anyone since the senior boss' secretary."

Lucy felt her eyes widen in surprise. "Really? Thank you, Carl. Any tips?"

"Take life as it comes, Miss. Don't over analyze it, take it personally, or worry over it. When the boss throws you a curve ball, just take your time, toss it back, and drink a mocha every now and again," he chuckled.

~

Jace paced the tarmac uncertain why it mattered so much for his new personal assistant to show. He glanced at his watch for the fifteenth time. He kicked himself for not showing at the staff meeting and wondered how it went. At least Lucy answered his call. The last assistant just left the company phone on her desk and walked out the office building never to return.

At the sight of the shiny black limo turning into the airport, he blew out the breath he'd been holding and sent up a prayer for help. His brain worked so fast he typically left everyone and every detail in the dust. Lucy's management style fit him perfectly... if he could keep from running her off.

The sleek limo came to a stop on the tarmac fifty feet from his plane. Jace tugged at the open collar of his wine silk shirt. Why did having Lucy show up mean so much? He shrugged it off, forced his hands behind his back and planted both feet in his usual confident stance. Anyone would be lucky to have this job; he reminded his wayward brain. His natural confidence rose to the surface and shoved all insecurities aside... until Lucy's long slender legs emerged from the limo. A lump formed in his throat. She'd arrived, on time, and... *with a smile on her face?*

He stopped his forward motion for half a heartbeat before snapping out of it and slapping grin on his face. With a nod toward the driver... why did he always forget the man's name? He turned toward his one hope for structure.

"Lucy..." he motioned toward the plane and

dug right in to the obvious. "Please accept my apologies. It is not everyday you get a call from the President of the United States' office. It sent my whole morning into a whirlwind."

He rubbed the back of his neck. "And although that's a great excuse, I wish I could say it's the exception. Somehow, it always ends up being the rule in my world." He paused. "How did the meeting go?"

She blew out a breath and nodded toward the plane. "Let's walk and talk. I don't want to make us late." Her long strides refreshingly matched his. "The meeting began slightly awkward until I took the bull by the horns." She paused and faced him.

"I hope you don't mind, but I told all your department heads that any requests for your time and attention funnels through me. They are generating department reports and requests as we speak. April, my assistant, will funnel all requests for your time to me as well, so we can get ahead of your schedule.

Anything of importance, I will bring to your attention, all reports will be reviewed by me and given to you. Otherwise, it is my goal to free you from the mundane daily details to do what you do best: create, invent, represent. Behind the scenes, I will consolidate, coordinate, stonewall, negotiate and protect."

She cocked her head and a moment of insecurity flashed in her deep blue eyes. A smile pulled at the corners of his mouth as relief washed over him. Finally! Someone who understood his needs.

"Miss Christianson, you are the first person to

truly understand what I need and step up to fill it. I bless the day we met." He bowed slightly and motioned for her to proceed him up the gangway. Her smile lit the afternoon sky at his praise. With a slight nod, she started up the stairs.

"And I praise God for that moment as well, Mr. Sheridan. You are a gift I didn't know I sought."

Chapter Four

The words of his new manager looped in Jace's overactive brain, resounding over again as he and Lucy stepped aboard the plane. No one, with the exception of his maternal grandfather, had ever called his challenging nature an opportunity, though many thought his money and power a gift. Lucy's words... he struggled to let them sink in. In his world, true praise baffled him. Raised by nannies, tolerated by busy parents and surrounded by greed: honest compassion kept him at a loss. He shoved the thought to the back of his mental playground for further analysis at a later date.

The President's daughter, Victoria, stood to greet them while his school chum, Jeff, turned high profile lawyer, lounged in a leather chair in his lazy, yet always charming way.

Turning to introduce Lucy, he caught a momentary look of appreciation flash across her face at the interior of his plane. Just as quickly as it appeared, it vanished, and the consummate professional reappeared. He glanced around his plane seeing it with new eyes. Eight leather lounge chairs placed in groupings of two or four surrounded mahogany coffee tables. A flight attendant waited in uniform near the front of the plane. Polished mahogany, etched glass and gold fixtures or trim spoke of opulence that he took for granted. Lucy's freshness forced him to see through different eyes.

"Miss Christianson, allow me to introduce Victoria Blaylock, an accomplished clean energy CEO in her own right. She is here to represent the President's position on a global scale."

Victoria sized up his assistant. Lucy stood her ground and nodded pleasantly with the same confident manner that caught him off guard the day they met. The woman acted like she'd been born to power. The President's daughter immediately picked up on her confidence and smiled.

"I like this one, Jace."

"It is a pleasure to meet you, Miss Christianson. Anyone who can keep Jace Sheridan on track is a highly accomplished woman." She casually took her seat. "You and I are not much different in our mission this trip. I represent the President and you represent, Mr. Sheridan. Please, let me know if I may answer any questions for you."

A curious light flickered in Lucy's blue eyes, yet she accepted the hand offered with a smile and a gracious word before turning to their other passenger. For some reason, the thought of introducing his new assistant to his old roommate made him cringe. It wouldn't be the first time Jeffery stole a lovely lady from under his very nose.

Before he could make the introduction, Jeff stood to his feet and bowed over Lucy's hand and kissed it. A feeling of delight coursed through his veins when she quickly retracted her hand.

"And who is this pretty lady, Jace? You neglected to introduce me…." The wolf in sheep's clothing grinned. "Jeffrey Cavanaugh at your service, Miss…"

Jace stepped closer and took ownership by placing a hand on Lucy's shoulder. "Jeff, this is my new *personal* manager, Lucy Christianson. Please put your tongue back in your head and show some respect. How is Cynthia?"

Jeff shot him an irritated look. "In Paris modeling this season's collection…" He took a step back and released Lucy's hand. Good, the man needed to realize women were more than notches on a belt. The two made eye contact. Jeff broke off first with a nod and stepped back to his window seat.

As the flight attendant stepped forward to offer drinks, Lucy followed him toward the two leather seats in a private grouping. Reaching for the belt, she fastened in for takeoff before turning a rather irritated, furrowed brow toward him.

"And just what, MR. Sheridan, did you mean by placing a hand on my shoulder. Did you believe I could not hold my own a moment ago? Law suits start with less…" Her voice held a mixture of curiosity and accusation.

Jace felt heat rise up the collar of his shirt to his neck. What *had* he been thinking? Honesty demanded he acknowledge the emotions driving many of his decisions as of late. How did he put into words the drive to protect his turf when threatened? He and Jeff circled like a pair of alphas: Jeff as a rogue, and he as a guardian.

Lucy tilted her head and studied him quietly awaiting his reply. He risked a glimpse at Jeff flirting with the flight attendant and took a deep breath.

"Miss Christianson," he chose the proper reference to her name. "The moment you came to work for me, you entered an old rivalry unawares. "Jeff's father and mine were friends, yet Jeff can only see me as heir to a dynasty and himself as somehow cheated in the role of legal counsel. At the risk of sounding antiquated, anything in my possession, he seeks to obtain. To him, fast cars, portfolios, real estate and women are all property.

My actions reminded him that I am the bigger dog, and he just stepped onto my turf." He crossed one leg over the other and steepled his fingers in thought.

"So why…

"…keep him around? There are two reasons: loyalty… my father took him in when his own father died, but the greatest reason… having an attack dog is a valuable asset, as long as I keep him on a lease. I apologize for causing you distress. I meant no disrespect to you."

The flight attendant stepped up and offered a variety of drinks. He requested a water with an aspirin to help his pounding headache. Lucy chose a raspberry ginger ale.

Everywhere he turned recently roadblocks and accidents occurred: like the recent oil fires or his lost invitation to the Geneva Summit. He closed his eyes and rubbed his temples. He'd been playing catchup since he awakened.

A soft voice summoned his attention. "Mr. Sheridan… Jace…" He blinked awake to Miss Christianson's soft smile and rubbed his five o'clock shadow.

"How long have I been out?" the gruffness of his deep voice startled him. He rubbed his hand over his face again. Miss Christianson's smile only deepened. Was the woman *never* rattled?

"Only five minutes. The attendant brought your aspirin. I thought perhaps you should take it, and since the competition seems to have settled in for a nap as well, I'd like a few undisturbed moments to discuss our strategy at the summit."

Jace popped the aspirin in his mouth and chugged half the water down after it before responding. "What strategy? I attend. I answer questions. I shake a few hands. We leave." He scanned her with a critical eye. "Oh, I hope you brought a gown because I'm expecting you to attend as my…"

"*Personal assistant…* I know, and *I am prepared*, but you need to be as well. That's why your staff is currently sending over a number of statistics and bullet points compiled from company data in the event we need to provide support for our present energy position. I also requested a power point presentation of the environmental and community programs in which Sheridan Energy participates, plus a number of great shots of you… with boots on the ground. I put out a call throughout the company, and your people responded."

She smiled and crossed her arms after handing him her personal device with the presentation. "You may feel the hurricane force winds swirling in your life, Mr. Sheridan, yet for those around you... you've been the eye in the storm. You've been busy helping, Jace. I'm just here to direct the sails. Your people adore you. They've sent in dozens of photos." She pointed to the device. "Take a look."

Stunned beyond words, Jace scrolled through the unedited photos. A myriad of shots lay documented before him. Pics caught on camera showed him running from the oil fire, carrying a terribly burned child. Another photo revealed him sitting cross-legged listening to an old woman. She'd shared her concerns, and her advice proved valuable. His assistance installing a new generator at one of the plants, and carrying the groceries of a pregnant employee he happened upon at the local drugstore; all were documented. Several pics represented his attendance at fundraisers and community barbeques. A well of emotion threatened to surface. He rubbed the back of his head and his eyes darted to hers in confusion.

"I just want to help. I don't do *this* for publicity," he insisted. "It's not about me. It's the people who make our company great that should be highlighted, Lucy."

"And we do have pics of your employees helping as well, but you are a light. You shine hope in dark hours. Not many billionaires show the same compassion when the camera lights turn off."

He shook his head in disparagement, his

laughter tinged with disbelief. "And what qualifies you to make such a statement. You know *so* many billionaires, Lucy."

She crossed her arms and gave him a look that made him question. "Do you?"

Her full rosy lips parted slightly as if about to answer. Just as quickly, she closed her mouth. Hollywood movies stars paid big money to imitate a full-lipped permanent pout. A mouth he shouldn't be noticing. He shook it off.

"Look, Lucy… Miss Christianson, I'm overwhelmed with your work. Somehow, you managed to intertwine statistics with heart. Thank you for the compliment. Give me time. I'm not used to sincerity. Make sure you buy something on me when we get to Geneva."

Her eyes twinkled. "I already did. You purchased for me: a lovely evening gown, a pair of earrings, shoes and a purse that is being delivered to our hotel as we speak."

He chuckled, leaned back and folded his arms. "Oh really? How is my taste in ladies evening fashion?"

"You'll find out tomorrow evening, but I will say, Mr. Sheridan… you have great taste."

"Of course, I do," he leaned forward and briefly touched the back of her hand. "I chose you, didn't I? Wake me twenty minutes before we land, in Warsaw, Miss Christianson. Excellent work today." He shut his eyes and lowered his voice. "I look forward to seeing the result of my great taste. By the way… what color gown did I chose?"

"Ice blue."

"Perfect. My favorite. Good night, Lucy."

"Wait, Warsaw? I thought we were flying to Geneva."

"We are." He spoke with his eyes still closed. "Just a quick vision trip with the Polish Minister of Energy. I mentioned it earlier. I'm meeting him briefly in the airport. You'll take notes, of course. Then its just a jump to Geneva. We'll still be there in time to dress for dinner..." His voice fell off as the man drifted into sleep.

Twenty minutes before landing, Jace excused himself to freshen up in his private quarters at the back of the plane, while she and the two other passengers received a light breakfast. The sky swirled with ominous gray clouds and a cold drizzle drummed a rhythm on the windows of the plane. Her once crisp business suit lay in wrinkles made worse after deplaning on the tarmac in the rain.

Everywhere Lucy looked, the world lacked the brightness of light and joy. Grey dominated the landscape from the continually overcast drizzle to the nondescript color and design of the buildings and furniture. Her Polish counterpart escorted them to a small, private conference room where the Minister of Energy shook Jace's hand. The two got down to business. The logistics and negotiations combined with her exhaustion from the non-stop schedule. She struggled to stifle a yawn. Jace caught her, raised an eyebrow and paused.

"Minister, we discussed a number of interesting options for our two nations today. I wonder if I may have the last ten minutes of your time without our assistants?"

The minister nodded, and Jace dismissed her with instruction to meet him at the departure gate. Gratitude at her boss' thoughtfulness resonated in her tired brain. She stumbled through the airport looking for anything to give her a burst of energy. A chai latte and a yogurt barely scratched the surface of her exhaustion. Head in hands, she studied the passersby. The attitude of the population carried a heaviness of heart that wore out the soul.

Jace strode up and tossed her a small package of dried sausages. Sausages? She shot him a startled glance. "What's this?" She turned the package over in her hand.

"An airport snack… It's better than it looks. Try it."

Flavor burst in her mouth at the first bite. "Mm… you're right. It is much better than it looks."

He sobered. "Appearances can be deceiving, Lucy. Look around. You see gloom and despair, yet I see an opportunity for the light and for hope. I enjoy taking Sheridan Energy to places needing hope."

She looked around with new vision. What if instead of seeing the gloom, despair and hopelessness around her, she saw an opportunity for the light? Turning new eyes to the dreamer beside her, she searched a tired face that willed her to understand. Someone needed to focus all Jace's energy and vision then turn him loose on the world.

"I need your help, Lucy," his deep voice rumbled in her ear in a declaration that sent tingles along her neck. *Hot and cold, visionary yet laser focused, jovial yet serious-minded: who is this man?* Her mental radar struggled to find a fixed point. What could he possibly mean? He interrupted her thoughts with a nod toward the Lear Jet.

Standing, he waited for her to follow his lead before continuing his unexpected line of thought. With furrowed brow, he turned to catch her eye while striding confidently through the long grey terminal.

Strong hands waved in the air showcasing his frustration. "In my mind, I see the individual pieces to an entire puzzle along with the big picture of the completed puzzle… all at the same time. My visions work… I've proven it time and again with any project I touch… until my father's old secretary died, and I discovered my biggest flaw."

He turned suddenly and threw both hands in the air. "I need an interpreter. Someone who can both understand my vision and in turn communicate or help me communicate the vision to those around me. The bullet points and reports the office sent over were brilliant. You focused my thoughts… ordered my passion by giving it feet on the solid ground of facts, typed out in a way I can communicate. Can you do it again?"

"Am I understanding you correctly when I say, you need me to catch your visions and put them into passionate, workable proposals?"

Jace's smile grew as wide as Texas. "Exactly!" he exclaimed. He motioned for her to proceed him onto the tarmac where the plane awaited their arrival.

Lucy swallowed hard against the lump in her throat. Catching her boss' vision meant getting close to his heart. Already, she felt her own heart pound when he called her name, and barely two weeks had passed. Getting her heart and his so closely entwined invited trouble. Her billionaire boss might need her skills in business, but more anymore risked her heart.

She glanced up ready to refuse to do more than organize his planner when his boyish eager eyes locked with her own. To some degree the strong alpha male held a hint of the vulnerable, something deeper… a magnetism that drew her closer still.

She blew out a sigh and held his eager gaze. "Do you understand what you are asking, boss? Letting me into your heart to the point I understand you fully is a job usually reserved for a spouse or a family member. Isn't there someone else?"

Sorrow flickered in his dark brown eyes. "Only my half-sister, and she's not interested in this business. It's not her family. Though the energy company is my hobby, I am also responsible to take care of my grandfather's interests and holdings for the family. I created the energy company to help my home country of Lichtnovia as well as bring hope to dark places."

"No fiancé, or sweetheart to share your dreams…?"

"None. Though many pose for the camera or feign interest, but they desire money and power. None care enough to listen."

Lucy stuck out her hand. "Well, boss, if you let me in… I'll do my best to jump in with both feet.

Just be careful you don't fall for me along the way," she teased. "It's bad for business."

Surprise lit a fire in his eyes along with a new awareness. She'd meant to lighten the load for her own heart. Instead, she felt a new warmth from the man. She should withdraw…

He took her hand and his eyes twinkled with wolfish humor. "Warning duly noted. Don't fall for my assistant. Then I'll issue a similar warning… Don't fall for the boss. Any aspirations to tame the eligible, reckless billionaire, Lucy?"

She raised an eyebrow and cocked her head, "Wouldn't dream of it, Sir… It just isn't done. Besides, I've already got access to your credit cards, planes, cars and mansions… a relationship would just complicate things. The only thing I don't have access to is your heart… and, oh that's right… you just offered to share that with me too."

She matched his sarcastic tone, winked and turned to board the plane. Jace Sheridan, billionaire bachelor stood frozen speechless below.

Jeff stood as she entered the plane and caught her eye. She narrowed her gaze and held his. He raised an eyebrow and a glass.

"Does Jace know what he's in for with you, Miss Christianson?" His voice held amusement.

"He knows," she countered as Jace stepped onto the plane, his eyes darting between the two. Jeff grinned. Jace's fierce eyes bored into his rival's before turning to meet hers. The swirl of emotion she met there took her breath away. With a nod, she excused herself for the ladies' room. Time… she needed a moment.

A few moments later, a soft rap on the bathroom door drew her out of her panic.

"Miss Christianson, Lucy? The soothing voice of the President's daughter eased her heart. She opened the door a crack.

"Yes?"

Victoria cocked her head in understanding. "The captain is ready for take off and would like us in our seats. Are you okay? I've known Jace since prep school, and I've never seen him so flustered."

Lucy stepped into the aisle and shut the door behind her. "Mr. Sheridan made a request that would require a deeper dive into his heart. I reminded him stepping up to the fine line between boss and sweetheart is a dangerous game that I'm not planning to play. He teased, but I think he must be used to being pursued. I told him I'd help, but walked away. That and the rivalry between he and his lawyer is... troubling."

Victoria nodded and led the way back to the main cabin. Just before taking her seat, she whispered. "Whether or not you are interested in pursuing Jace, Miss Christianson, that little move captivated him. Guard your heart if you want to keep it. Once committed, Jace Sheridan doesn't like to lose."

"Then it's a good thing I don't play games," she smiled at Victoria and the woman tipped an invisible hat. "I wish you the best of luck with that, dear," she chuckled. "The more you run, the more he'll pursue. May I ask why you aren't interested?"

Lucy bit her lip. Having a friend to confide in would be a blessing, but convention dictated discretion. "It's complicated." She answered simply.

"Great romances always are, Miss Christianson." Victoria jerked her head toward the cabin. "Shall we?"

Lucy followed her and took her seat. Turning her body away from Jace, she sucked in a slow, deep breath and forced her tired body to relax in the comfortable leather recliner. Closing her eyes, she fell fast asleep.

Jace steepled his fingers and watched his new assistant nap. His skills as a host failed miserably this trip. At least Victoria and Jeffery occupied themselves with movies and music. His mood fluctuated every few moments. Lucy baffled him, intrigued him. She embodied the anti-flirt. After only a week, her organized, indomitable spirit soothed and refreshed him, yet her take him or leave him attitude boggled his mind.

Her previous salary must have paled in comparison to what he paid her now, but she appeared to enjoy the same level of contentment in either position.

If she doesn't care about the money or power, what does she care about? he wondered. The question intrigued him. *In fact, if money and power mean little to her, what do I mean to her? Strip away the billions and the influential people around me and... who am I?*

Like most teen heirs to billions, he's attended the Sacred Heart Boarding School, tried a stint at acting, headed up a few global initiatives to save the oceans, the rainforest and other well-intentioned attempts to add meaning to life, before taking the helm of his grandfather's business interests and starting his own energy company.

Standing, he headed to his private bath to shave. He stared into the mirror at the man reflecting back. Women rarely saw past the carefully crafted five o'clock shadow and padded wallet. What did Lucy see? Placing his hands on the marble counter, he shut his eyes and tried to see through her eyes. A vision of the dirty, clumsy biker entered his mind's eye.

Lucy treated him with dignity before he offered her the job of a lifetime. In fact, everyone around her received similar treatment. Limo driver or billionaire, all received the kind attention of his assistant, and he needed to know why. Splashing water on his face, he made quick work of taming *the shadow* as he jokingly called his annoying facial hair, changed into the casual track suit he kept aboard for long flights, and stepped back into the main cabin.

I'll get to the heart of what makes Lucy tick before the flight is over, he decided, but the time never arrived. His assistant slept the rest of the flight.

Chapter Five

Lucy screamed into her plump, hotel room pillow. Seven hours until the Geneva Summit ball and her missing dress still refused to materialize. After calling for the last two days, no one could nail down the location. Meetings, details, connections were all finalized, leaving a whole afternoon for relaxation and preparation before the grand finale gala, yet here she sat without a dress. Her lower lip protruded in a grand pout. A knock sounded on her hotel room door.

She yanked it open, hoping for a miracle... Jace stood dazed with one fist in the air ready to knock again. Dressed in street clothes, he took one look at her fuzzy pajama pants and stepped back.

"Whoa, I, uh... wondered if you need to stretch your legs and see a few sights other than conference rooms, but I see you are planning a restful afternoon," he managed.

"Hardly! My gown vanished into thin air along with its accessories." She threw her hands in the air out of frustration. "I took care of this a week ago, but there is no accounting for international delivery services, I suppose. I'm at a loss."

Jace raised an eyebrow, crossed his arms and grinned. "Well, this is something new. The unflappable Miss Christianson in the midst of a crisis. Need my help?"

Lucy opened the door wider for him and retreated to the sofa. Grabbing a pillow, she plopped down. "Please! Ideas?"

He sat down across from her and steepled his fingers in thought. "We can handle this crisis one of two ways," he began. "First, call the manager of the hotel with your sizes and have him send up two or three options. They offer specialized service to high profile clients, so I'm certain we qualify."

Lucy shifted in her seat on the green couch. "I feel a bit uncomfortable having a stranger pick out my clothes. What is your other option?" she entreated.

Jace leaned forward from his position across from hers. "Change clothes. Meet me downstairs in fifteen minutes. I know a couple of men's shops in the area which are combined with women's clothing. I say we run over, find what you need, grab a pastry, see a sight or two and be back in time to change for the event."

Lucy jumped to her feet. "Let's do it!" She hesitated. "Are you certain you want to come with me? You could just send me in the right direction, Boss." She emphasized his title. His dark eyes narrowed.

"I invited *you*, remember? I'll see you downstairs…" He glanced at his watch. "…in fifteen minutes. Don't be late," he snapped.

Brushing off Jace's irritation, Lucy sped into action. She stared at her open bag hoping something among her limited outfits would jump out at her. She sighed. When Jace said the family butler packed her suitcase, only an overnight bag containing a pair of black slacks and a couple of shirts made the flight. The whirlwind pace offered no time to purchase a new wardrobe. A leopard print blouse peeked out from beneath her standard black slacks. Done.

Adding low heels, a wine shade of lipstick and gold hoops; she coiled her long blond hair into a French Twist. A final glance in the mirror confirmed her fears… pretty, not glamourous enough for a Geneva outing with the billionaire bachelor. Shrugging it off, she grabbed her black handbag and made it to the lobby with one minute to spare. Jace stood pacing in the corner. His face brightened the moment their eyes locked.

"Thought perhaps you changed your mind and decided on Plan A." His husky voice held an unknown emotion. She shook her head and smiled.

"Not on your life, Boss. I thought *you* might want the out. After all, the afternoon is empty. The world awaits."

He held the hotel door open for her, and they stepped out onto the street before he answered. "Geneva is better seen with a friend. Come. The shop is just around the corner."

Five minutes later, they stepped into a small boutique. Custom gowns of every design shimmered in a rainbow of colors. Through an arched doorway, custom suits and tuxedos graced the next room.

Her fingers itched to touch the silks and organdies. Gemstones and accessories sparkled in gilded glass cases. She turned to her billionaire boss to find him studying her with a raised eyebrow.

"Go play, Lucy. The owner is a friend."

"But, Mr. Sheridan…"

He turned back and cocked his dark head clearly irritated at her formal use of his name.

"Yes…"

She tilted her head and studied him.

"Well, what is it?" Impatience tinged his deep voice.

She dared to step forward and whisper. "Who's buying?"

His brow furrowed in confusion. He cleared his throat. "Perhaps I didn't make myself clear. We are shopping for you this afternoon. I mentioned when I brought you on that you would need certain upgrades in your wardrobe. This is the first chance we've had to rectify the situation."

He paused to let his words sink in. She took a moment to process, then spun in a circle, taking in the room. He rested his hands on her shoulders.

"Miss Christianson, you are under my care, and I take care of what's mine," he growled with a tinge of frustration. "Did you think otherwise?"

He snapped his fingers and the sharply dressed owner came running.

"George, this is my very reluctant assistant. She needs… everything. An evening gown for tonight with all the accessories plus several more for events of the season. Take care of her. I'm stepping out for a moment. Oh… and George, we're going for elegant, and I'm partial to ice blue for tonight's occasion."

The man nodded and scurried through a back door in the establishment clapping his hands furiously. Lucy stared after him. She turned toward her benefactor and opened her mouth to speak. He placed a finger over her lips.

"He'll be back and take care of everything, Lucy. Just… be the light that you are. I'll return in an hour."

"You're leaving? What's my budget?" It was a test really… she knew his answer before he spoke it aloud, but the question needed asking. Trust must develop between them if her undertaking with Jace were to succeed.

He tapped her nose and chuckled. "This must be a whole new world for you, my shy assistant. I rather like it. Finally, you need me." He leaned close and whispered in her ear. "There is *no budget,* Lucy, darling. Welcome to the billionaire bachelor club. There are only eight of us in the world you know, and I have no one to personally spend on. I have my favorite charities, but no one in my life. My half-sister and I just met two years ago. She spends her own fortune. Allow me a little fun, will you?"

Pleased, she nodded as Jace strode confidently out the door. A rush of attendants covered in sparkling ice blue poured out of the simple back door. George ushered her to a lush private screening room and a comfortable chair as the models lined up on a carpeted platform. A lovely redhead offered a raspberry ginger ale, her favorite, on a silver platter. A clap of the hands set the ladies in motion modeling the various styles available for her favorite ice blue. Varying lengths, varying degrees of décolletage, long sleeves, short sleeves, draped sleeves, off the shoulder. The endless choices overwhelmed: lace, tulle, embroidery, satin, silk...

"See what you like, Mademoiselle?" George's monotone voice insisted she make a choice. The models lined up across the stage and around the room in graceful positions. Two ice blue gowns stood out and one in silver.

"Perhaps I might try those three?" She nodded in a self-assured manner. Alone, she could shine. Being without her real wardrobe for nearly two weeks felt like entering battle without her armor.

George clapped his hands in the air before motioning the three models to step forward. He leaned forward with an air of concern.

"But mademoiselle, I am not certain how the silver gown ended up in the fashion show today. Monsieur implicitly requested ice blue."

Her confidence rose to the forefront and a giggle bubbled forth. "That is because, Monsieur George, my boss knows *I* love ice blue. My original ice blue gown disappeared among the postal service. Mr. Sheridan leaves nothing to chance in finding another gown to suit, but my assistant April ordered the original at *my* request. I..."

George staggered back dramatically and slapped his forehead. "April, you say..."

She nodded in surprise. Could he have found

her gown?

"Yes. My assistant ordered the gown from a local shop, since our schedule filled so rapidly."

Waving his hands in the air and speaking rapidly in French, George turned to his quiet assistant and barked instructions. Turning back with an apologetic glance, he snatched up her hands and covered them with his own.

"My apologies, my lady. I know this dress. The mail service returned it this morning. My assistant is hanging it in the dressing room now for your approval. In the meantime, would one of these others still interest you? Or something in another color, perhaps? The shoes and handbag are a gift for your trouble. Now, Monsieur Sheridan insisted I take care of you with several gowns."

His hand swept the room where the models stood waiting.

"The floor-length, silver embroidered gown with the silver flutter sleeves and layers of tiered tulle shimmers in the light. It's magical."

He snapped his fingers and the model approached gracefully with a slow turn. Lucy examined it with a detailed eye. A slow smile lit George's face.

"Aww… you know fashion, yes?" He cocked his head in thought. "Perhaps you have done this before?" For one moment, he paused, "May I inquire you name again, Mademoiselle?

Lucy smiled. "Lucinda Christianson."

The man opened and shut his mouth like a fish out of water. "Would you perhaps be related to…?"

She held up her hand to stop his question. "You

may know of my cousin David from Jublanovia, but J'ai besoin de votre discrétion oui?" She whispered in French and then reiterated in English. "I need your discretion. Mr. Sheridan enlisted my assistance believing me to be a personal assistant. Having had one of my own all my life, I am helping order his world... as a friend. Oui?"

George eyed her for one moment before agreeing, something she appreciated.

"Oui, Mademoiselle... how very romantic," he winked. "Now, we will send this to try." His nod sent the model scurrying out of the room. He rubbed eager hands together. "Now, what else. You need at least two others."

"The ice blue with the floor length A-line silk skirt, embroidered bodice and collar, with the low back gleams, but the simple off the shoulder tulle dress with an over lay of crystal beads and white embroidery with cape sleeves reminds me of a fairy-tale. What are your thoughts, George?"

The man beamed at her inquiry. "Will this dress be for business or pleasure?"

Lucy's eyes shot to meet the man's hawkeyed gaze. She hesitated. "Business... I suppose," she stammered.

"I see... if for business, the A-line silk is perfection, but if perhaps, you anticipate a fairy-tale evening... the fluttery tulle with draped sleeves. Might I suggest you try the A-line in a wine color and purchase the fairy-tale ice blue for a special occasion." He leaned in close enough to smell the peppermint on his breath.

"I happen to know that every year Monsieur

Sheridan receives an invitation which he refuses. Perhaps the venue might interest you" He waved his handkerchief. "Mr. Sheridan is distant cousin to a number of royal families, yet rarely accepts an invitation since the death of his parents. I digress..." he shook his head and offered his hand to help her rise.

"My point, imagine the fairy-tale dress under the stars at the Jublanovian Palace on Christmas Eve. Perhaps this year your boss might be convinced to go. There are those who would see him emerge from his cocoon of mourning and hard work to join the world stage. Come. Try on the dresses..."

An hour later, exhausted and starving, she fell back into a brocaded mahogany chair and stared wide-eyed at the glorious bits and bobs George passionately insisted belonged with the *four* evening gowns. She felt a headache coming on. Imagining the exurbanite cost of this shopping spree most certainly caused it. What would Jace say? She didn't have long to find out.

The hunk of a man breezed into the shop, arched an amused brow at her exhausted posture, and scanned the purchases. Immediately, he began to argue in French. Lucy felt her upper back muscles tense and the back of her head tightened increasing her headache. She rubbed her eyebrows to relieve the tension. The arguing increased, yet she forced herself to stay composed in the presence of her boss.

Wonder and disbelief danced in her tired mind as George scrambled to pull precious gems from three cases and lay them before Jace. The powerful gentleman commanded attention in his own unique, unaffected manner. She scrambled to his side. She didn't need all that George insisted she purchase.

"Mr. Sheridan, Jace…" she whispered. "This is too much. George encouraged four gowns with all the accessories. I assured him you did not authorize such expenditures. Please, jewelry… a woman aught not receive jewelry from anyone but her man. It is too much."

Jace stilled, and his dark eyes searched her ice blues before narrowing. With his back to the counter, he held up his hand. George paused and darted a glance between the two of them. "A moment with the lady, George," he spoke without losing her eye contact. George scrambled from the room along with his assistants.

"Miss Christianson, you shame me. I do *not* want to hear the excuses again. To have you appear at my side without the trappings of the uber rich will dishonor me. Unfortunately, in this class, people are measured by the power, possessions and beauty at our beck and call.

Beauty is a gift that must be cultivated just like brains. Why do you hesitate to use it for good? It draws others to you. Beautiful gardens take generations to master. Beautiful clothing starts with a single silk worm and takes master designers to create. A beautiful body requires nutrition, discipline and care.

I am not here to exploit you. Since I hired you for your many gifts, it is my responsibility to provide the tools to thrive in this world. If I offer jewels, gowns and glass slippers… be like Cinderella and humbly accept or leave my employ, but do not insult my honor again. If I were making an inappropriate move, you would know it by now. I am *not* the man the magazines strive to create." He lowered his voice to a gentle whisper. "Allow me to do this for you."

Lucy's eyes welled with legitimate tears. Jace was right to be frustrated. She wished she could explain that she possessed several closets full of equally lovely gowns and an arsenal of jewels, but the timing… to protest further robbed George of a sale and Jace of his dignity. She did recognize an honorable man. All he'd asked for in return for a generous salary was a visionary manager to help cast his vision to people of influence.

Leaning against the glass jewelry case, he crossed powerful arms across his chest. Goodness, the man worked out. The muscles, five o'clock shadow, black silk open necked shirt combined with his sudden commanding intensity left her breathless. The alpha male awaited her response. Jace's magnetism drew her like a moth to a flame, but more importantly, the heart behind it cried out to her.

A world of beauty, power, influence shimmered. She only needed to reach out and embrace the role. Be the power behind the power, be the neck that turns the head… Ahh… the familiar role beckoned, a part she'd continually resisted until this moment.

Lifting her eyes to meet his, she managed a smile. He calmly lifted one eyebrow and uncrossed his arms.

"Forgive me, Mr. Sheridan… Jace. I accept your offer and thank you for the explanation. I only have one thing to ask?"

Her billionaire nodded and checked his watch. "What is it?"

"May I have a tiara? I wouldn't want to shame you…" She purposely widened her eyes to create an innocent, girlish aura and added a tiny pout and an eyelash flutter to top it off.

Caught off guard, Jace blinked. Chuckling under his breath, he clapped his hands for George and the staff to return. "George… the lady needs a tiara and spare no expense."

He chucked her under the chin and winked. "You are terrible at the vixen pout, you know that? Anything else while you have my attention?"

She affected a lower lip pout, "Well, perhaps a mink coat would do…"

He burst out laughing and raised his hand to summon help. She hurriedly grabbed it out of the air. "Jace… I'm kidding. Why do I need a fur coat?"

"Be…cause it's currently winter, almost Christmas, and I thought we'd visit the capital of Jublanovia one day. George… bring your top two fur coats. One real fur and one faux."

She momentarily froze at his mention of Jublanovia. Five minutes later, the furs were added to the growing pile. Lucy tugged on Jace's sleeve. "Boss… I'm starving. All this shopping is exhausting. I don't suppose you have any money left for coffee and that pastry we discussed earlier? If not, I'm buying. Just please… feed me!" she begged.

He grinned. "Okay George, we wore the lady out. Until next time, my friend." The two men shook hands. George promised to deliver things to immediately to the hotel. Jace gently placed his hand to the small of her back and ushered her out onto the street.

Chapter Six

Since when had tying a necktie become so challenging? Jace wondered. He knew when... ever since Lucy Christianson joined his staff, his world upended. He chuckled at the memory of her response to his ultimatum. Somehow, the unexperienced woman bowed to his wisdom, learned her lesson, created laughter out of a tense moment, and ended up with a diamond tiara and two fur coats to boot!

He rarely spent money on anything personal these days. Hearing Lucy's insistence of her minimal needs offered a refreshing change from the hangers on who hoped for a few diamonds sprinkled their way. His heart pounded in his chest at the thought of seeing her in his purchases. He shook off the feeling. Lucy worked for him.

As an assistant, she's perfect, but as anything more? Jace, get a grip. You know the family rules. Being a quiet part of the royal lineup requires your bride to meet certain requirements. Lucy, as far as he knew, didn't fulfill any of them.

The sobering thought cleared his brain. He had to be careful. *Currently, there are only 43 families I am allowed to marry into without being disinherited,* he groaned. Sheridan Energy and Tech provided him with an important hobby, but diplomacy was the real family business. His grandfather might be a deposed king, but the man still worked tirelessly to help the fledgling democracy's struggling economy. Jace's energy company created jobs to that end.

Lucy... Miss Christianson, he reminded himself, might be a genuine person whose company he presently enjoyed, but people often were not what they seemed. In his spontaneity, he'd neglected to have a full workup done on her background.

Picking up a cell phone he rarely used, he pressed speed dial and requested a very detailed background check. The request set a whirlwind into motion with his grandparent's staff. He'd only requested the workup twice. Each time for a potential spouse. This time...

"No, Jacques, this is not for a bride. It's for a personal manager of my schedule. Yes, I know she's a woman! It's not like that!" He sighed. "Just run the full workup. Miss Lucy Danae Christianson. Yes, Christianson... Why is that interesting? You have got to be kidding me. Go ahead... do the full workup. If it turns out she's of the right family... well, I look forward to hearing the results."

The phone slipped out of his fingers as Jace let his man's words sink in. A chance... a slim one. According to Jacque, last year a forty-fourth acceptable family became accepted on the list: the extended Christianson royal family of Jublanovia. Could Lucy be eligible after all? If so, why would she be managing a convenience store? He thought back to the day he bumped into her.

Come to think of it, he never saw her in a uniform. Her lack of awe at his estate, her contentment with the salary package, her ability to stand toe to toe with him and her ability to resist the temptation to fall for a billionaire… it all suggested someone born to wealth and power. He ran his fingers through his dark hair and folded them at the back of his head as he paced the room. If Lucy belonged to the royal Christianson family, why would she accept his job offer?

He shook his head. Despite the breadcrumb of clues, the ridiculous idea couldn't be true, and yet…The despair that hovered like a dark cloud only a moment ago now parted with the dawn of a single ray of hope. He slammed the door on his fledgling desires. Jacque would take his time creating a complete workup. If… the door opened, he would see where it led. Until that time… he straightened his black silk tie, he would do his diplomatic part.

The tie felt tight. Duty choked the hope and breath out of him. He needed to get away from business, from tradition. He could not remember the last time he'd sloughed off everyone's expectations and taken a vacation. Jeffery and Victoria both planned to remain in Geneva.

What if he skipped the ball tonight altogether? He shoved the idea aside, but the thought refused to leave as he gelled his dark hair. Inspiration struck, and he picked up the phone to contact his pilot. Five minutes later, he slipped on his tuxedo jacket and dialed Lucy's suite down the hall. As usual, she answered his call immediately.

"What's up, boss?"

He chuckled at the idea of Lucy related to a royal house. "Are your bags packed, Miss Christianson?"

"At the rate you travel…? Always. Why?"

"We'll make an appearance at the ball and blow this joint after an hour. Tell your maid to pack the bags and have them delivered to the plane. I'll be right over to escort you downstairs."

Her voice broke as she squeaked into the phone. "Me? You're escorting me to the ball? Why? What happened to the President's daughter?" Skepticism tinged her usually confident, lighthearted tone.

"The President's daughter and Jeffery seemed to hit it off. It appears I am left without a date to the ball, fair lady. Would you do me the honor of filling in this once?" Silence met his request. Every other woman jumped at the chance. His ego took a hit.

"Miss Christianson…"

"I don't know, boss. If I arrive on your arm, I'll be in the limelight. You are always in the crosshairs of the media. I prefer to stay off their radar."

Alarm bells sounded in his head. If his Lucy belonged to the royal house of Jublanovia and appeared on his arm at the Geneva Summit, the press would light a fire worldwide. He stepped out the door and silently navigated the hallway to her suite.

"Lucy... open the door. I'm outside your suite."

"But... the stylist is here finishing my hair..."

Stylist? "Dismiss her and open the door."

"Five minutes?" she begged softly.

He checked his watch and began to pace, his mind spinning with 'what ifs'. "Five minutes, no more."

Four and a half minutes later, the door opened and a flustered hairstylist complete with her tools of the trade scurried out the door.

"Come in..." Lucy's voice echoed from the bedroom. "I'll be right out. What is all the fuss about, Mr. Sheridan?"

She stepped from the bedroom into the living area of the suite and took his breath away. The personal assistant he hired out of a gas station vanished and an elegant blonde in a figure-hugging, wine colored, floor-length gown stepped into view.

"Wow... forgive me, Miss Christianson, but you look lovely. I expected ice-blue..."

Her full lips curved into a quiet smile. "I changed my mind when you called. If we are just making a brief appearance, I'll save the blue for a special occasion. What is so urgent?" She motioned to the lovely seating area and gracefully took a seat.

He shook off the stupor he felt at seeing her in the new gown and joined her. "I need to get away. Now. All work and no play make Jace a dull boy." He rubbed the back of his neck and tried to explain.

"Mountains, vineyards or beaches?"

She blinked. "Excuse me?"

"for a vacation destination... I'm exhausted, and I can see the schedule wearing on you."

Understanding registered in her eyes. A mischievous twinkle followed.

"You received an invitation to the annual Jublanovian Royal Christmas Ball. Jublanovian skiing ranks as the world's finest and the cocoa is divine…" she offered with a look of innocence that made his pulse race. If Jacques' suspicions turned true the woman before him could belong to him with a word. The Jublanovian house and his own needed a match. He shut his eyes in confusion.

Why would Lucy keep the truth from him? Were they not on equal footing, both heirs of massive fortunes and a few steps away from the throne? Why do the work of a personal assistant when more than likely she had servants at her beck and call? Her insistence that she didn't need the gowns he offered registered.

"We're skipping the Geneva ball. Change clothes and meet me at the plane. The driver will be waiting," he barked.

Lucy's eyes flashed at his commanding tone, but he steeled his heart against her fire. Countless women toyed with his affections over the years, but none confused him more than the woman before him. With Lucy, he'd been vulnerable. He paced the room in frustration.

A cell phone pinged… hers. Lucy bent and slipped her slender fingers around the bright yellow case. Whatever flashed on the screen effected a small gasp from her otherwise composed demeanor.

Her blue eyes clouded with alarm and shot to meet his own. Hand to her mouth, she gathered her skirts and fled, abandoning him to rant alone.

Chapter Seven

Lucy panicked. She dialed the number on the screen, immediately relieved when Krister answered.

"Please, Krister, explain... A situation is exploding in the other room."

The smooth baritone of the family manager calmed the swirl of emotions raised by his call and Jace's strange behavior.

"I received a discreet call from the Habsperg royal family manager today requesting an inquiry into family members of the royal Christianson family, specifically a Lucy Christianson, my lady."

"The Habsperg family... whatever do they want from me and how would they know that designation?"

"It appears that though they are currently without a throne, they are not without a royal line. The youngest daughter of the toppled royal generation had a son. Three other grandsons and an uncle precede this young man as successors, but as fifth in line, he is required to marry among the forty-four acceptable royal lines.

An hour ago, that young man, a certain Jacian Augustus Habsperg Sheridan requested a much overdue work-up on his personal manager, a Miss Lucy Christianson. I'm to get back to his man in an hour. That's all the time he would give me."

Lucy sank into the pristine down comforter of her bed and cradled her head in her hands. "What does he know, Krister? It matters."

"The manager is hopeful in his suspicions that you are of the royal house of Christianson. He privately hinted that his master sounded the happiest he's heard him since the death of his parents. He carries the weight of all the Habsperg family interests. Everyone else in the family spends money. Your Mr. Sheridan is upholding his family. Jacque, the family manager mentioned his suspicions to Mr. Sheridan, who promptly insisted on the full work-up given to potential mates. I'm under the impression that Mr. Sheridan does not expect his manager's speculations to bear fruit.

I ask again, your royal highness, how may I assist in the matter? What are your wishes?"

Lucy set the phone on the bed and felt a thrill. For years she'd fought against the strict rule of marriage within the royal families to no avail, but after getting to know Jace…

She snatched up the phone as a plan entered her churning brain. "Tell him the truth, Krister, and ask for a similar background on Mr. Sheridan. Any union will need to be approved by my cousin, so would you let David know that as per his instructions, I'm *finally* interested in pursuing a match? I must know if he approves before I reveal myself. Make it clear to the Habsperg manager, that he is to keep his suspicions to himself if he has any hopes of making a match."

"Yes, your highness. I'm meeting the king in two hours. I'll make this a top priority and should have the information to present him upon our meeting. When would you like me to contact you?"

Lucy folded her hands to her chest in excitement. "As soon as possible, Krister."

She hung up and dialed the number of Jace's pilot. "Andrew, this is Miss Christianson. Mr. Sheridan suggested I choose the flight destination." She gave him the details, then rang up the maid. She'd kept her identity confined to a personal assistant of her own, but with her identity revealed, she intended to pull out all the stops.

With no idea of Jace's whereabouts or state of mind, she proceeded to change into elegant travel clothes worthy of a princess.

Thank you, George for throwing in a few extras.

Her hair and makeup already fit the persona of a princess. Lucy's association with Jace fell into the business category. He knew little about her. That was about to change.

The plane engine roared during takeoff. Jace stared out the window into a crystal blue sky uncertain where his anger should be directed. Seated across from him, Lucy typed on her personal device looking every inch a member of a royal house. Despite the message that sent her into a panic, she now radiated calm confidence. Ignoring his mood, she simply smiled.

Now, what? He wondered. Had he overreacted to her request for skiing in Jublanovia? His heart pounded in his chest at the thought that his hire might be eligible for his consideration. He understood her need to live a normal life or keep her identity under wraps, but why help him? Did she need access to his billions? A quick search on the royal Jublanovia family showed their net worth exceeding his own… Why would a princess mask herself as his personal assistant? She had no need for money, influence or power.

His schedule ran her ragged. He'd tracked the destination to which the company sent her weekly checks… a different orphanage received the funds both times. Other than dresses she didn't need, in return for her labors to bring order and peace to his world, she received nothing for herself. Why?

Oh God… if You are out there… I need to understand. I've given her nothing, yet she's given me everything.

You are loved, my son.

He buried his head in his hands and struggled to believe. Money and power never bought his parent's time or approval, never stopped the manipulation of cruel nannies. Stripped of it all, he fought to find value in the man in the mirror. What did Lucy see? Why was she here?

Ask her.

He heard the words loud and clear… then shoved them away until she looked over at him. Her lips parted in her permanent pout… one he now recognized. He stood and crossed the aisle. Her curious blue eyes followed him as he positioned himself so close his knees touched hers. Reaching out, he ran a finger across her full rosy lips. They parted in a gasp beneath his touch. She jerked back and slapped his hand bringing him back to reality.

"Lucy… I apologize," he stammered. "I just… I've been fascinated by your lips. People pay good money for what God gave you naturally, but I just realized where I've seen that attribute before. I got lost in my revelation," his voice filled with raw emotion at his lame apology.

She leaned her blonde head back against the recliner and crossed her arms. "Do tell, Mr. Sheridan… I'm fascinated." Sarcasm dripped from her voice once more. "Where have you seen my *lips* before?'

He pulled out his phone and held out a pic for her perusal. "On Marie Antoinette… though some family members were cursed with a severe affectation, Antoinette's jaw gave her the look of a permanent vixen pout. Are you related?" He awaited her answer with bated breath.

She shut her eyes and nodded. "Very distantly… yes."

He bit his lip and plunged forward. "I am mildly color blind for a similar familial reason. Early today, I took belated steps to run your background check. I'm terrible about such precautions. I've yet to hear back, but the family manager, Jacque suggested you might be related to the Christianson's of Jublanovia. I admit to being thrown into a tailspin. I don't like being in the dark.

When you suggested skiing in Jublanovia… I

exploded, felt both betrayed and hopeful. I feel a connection with you. Please forgive my harsh outburst. I'm not given to them, I promise."

She blinked. "I received a text from my family manager about your request. I panicked."

He leaned forward and nudged her knee with his own. "Who are you, Lucy?"

"That is a complicated question, boss. The day we bumped into one another at the convenience store, I arrived to check on a young woman I recommended for a job. You mistook me for the manager. I truly didn't recognize you at first, but when you told me your name, and offered me a position, I almost turned away. God stopped me. Told me to help bring peace to your world. I didn't need the money or position, but I've enjoyed getting to know the real Jace Sheridan, the man behind the money, without all the hype."

He rubbed a hand over his five o'clock shadow. "Tell me what you see, Lucy? The man behind the money and power... who do you see?"

Blue eyes brightened as she studied him a moment. He loved how she took time to think before leaping, unlike his spontaneous nature. "I see a man who needs peace and joy. A man who could set the world ablaze with light and hope... a hardworking, tireless man who needs someone by his side."

He cocked his head. "Do you still want the job, Lucy?"

She raised a well-groomed brow and offered the hint of a smile. "That remains to be seen."

Two hours later, when the plane came to a stop,

Jace followed Lucy off the plane. He blinked uncertain of his surroundings. Snow capped mountains graced the crystal blue sky. The destination should have been the Greek islands on the Mediterranean Sea.

"Lucy..." he barked. "Where are we?

She pulled the pins from her blonde updo allowing the silky lengths of her hair to fall in waves down her back. Spinning on her heels, she turned to face him and walked backward toward a flaming red Corvette C8. She spread her hands and lifted her face to the cloudless sky.

"Welcome to the home of my birth, boss... Jublanovia. You need a bit of adventure away from the cameras, and I can provide it. Oh, I forgot to ask... do you ski," her lips turned up in a cheerful smile revealing beautiful white teeth behind her full lips.

Jace filled his lungs with the crisp air. The last time he'd done anything fun...? Buying Lucy clothes came to mind, but a real vacation? He drew a blank.

"I've never taken the time to learn, but there is a first time for everything."

She walked backwards while chattering cheerfully. Glimpses of *this* Lucy, free and joyful shone through on rare occasions like riding in his fast car, or at the sight of a sparkling tiara. He suddenly felt the tension in his shoulders from years of public service and leadership. Other billionaires lived playboy lives. He shook his head unable to see himself in that role. The thought reminded him of the office back home and panic rose.

"Miss Christianson, who is taking the lead back home while I'm away?" He hated the tension in his voice. He truly needed the time away.

Reaching into her leather briefcase, she pulled out a slip of paper and met his eyes with a shrug. "I took the liberty of reorganizing the chain of command to streamline the business and free up your time. It only awaits your approval. Your staff appears pleased and willing to handle the changes if you agree."

His dark eyes scanned the terms and assignations of each department. "Lucy... Miss Christianson, this is brilliant. The company will run like clockwork while I'm away, leaving only the biggest decisions to me. You even assigned a rotation of company inspections? Thank you. This company started as a hobby, but such rapid growth made time for restructuring nearly impossible. We've needed this for so long. Now, I can pursue the family interests or even sell off the company!"

His eyes never left the paper as she opened the passenger door. "Restructuring approved, Miss Christianson." Looking up from the paper, he studied the car and grinned. "Let me guess... yours?" She winked. "I'm driving. Hop in."

She peeled out of the parking lot, putting a grin on his face, but twenty minutes later, he fell fast asleep.

Lucy's phone vibrated with a simple message.

"King David approves a match with Mr. Jacian Habsperg Sheridan."

Her phone vibrated again, this time with an

incoming call from her cousin.

"Can't wait to meet him. Krister is working with his people. Announcement to be made at the Christmas ball."

Her heart pounded in her chest, and heat pumped through her veins at the rapid turn of events. She chuckled under her breath and studied the exhausted form of her billionaire boss sleeping in the leather passenger seat. Her plan to lift his burdens and whisk him away for a quick vacation needed adjusting. The adventure ahead would either overtake them both, or they would enjoy the thrill of the ride.

Her Jace knew nothing. She hoped he would be pleased. An inspiration struck. She sent a quiet text and received a phone number in return. With a quick glance at the sleeping man across from her, she told her car to dial. The person on the other end picked up immediately.

"Jacque? This is Miss Lucy Christianson. For now, that designation will do, understood?"

The man on the other end hesitated, but agreed.

"What may I do for you, ma'am," Jacque stammered.

"I'd like your advice. Currently, the gentleman in question is asleep in the car, so forgive me if my voice is quiet. I am not quite ready to explain my position to our mutual friend here, but I have no desire for him to feel ambushed either. He is exhausted beyond belief from years of holding family and business together."

"Indeed, he is ma'am. We've all seen it, but there's been no help for it. Your insight and action on his behalf is noted and appreciated. How many I help?"

"A personal question first, Jacque. Has your boss expressed an interest in me beyond my role as his assistant?"

"Master Jace keeps his own council, Ma'am, but he's only asked for a background workup for a person of interest."

"Thank you. If my plan backfires, I will send him to you as a witness that I called because I care. I wish to reveal the joining of our houses just before the ball. I need time for him to get to know me. How is he with surprises?"

"You know him, Miss… he's the king of spontaneity."

She hung up the phone just as they arrived at Christianson Mountain Lodge. She nudged Jace awake. He ran a hand over his sleepy face in attempt to wake up. Stepping into the lodge together, she watched his face. A roaring fire in a ten-foot hearth blazed and crackled casting warmth and joy throughout the room. A gourmet cocoa and coffee bar beckoned. The valet nodded and directed their bags to the upper floor of suites.

Slipping her hand through Jace's arm, she tugged him toward the cocoa. He beamed down at her face. "Okay, Miss Christianson…"

"Lucy…" she insisted for the first time.

His raised his brows in questioning surprise. "Lucy, is it now…?" He affected a mock bow. "Lucy…" he began again. "show me your world."

The next morning, Jace regretted he'd ever said those words. *Add world class skiing to the list of my enigmatic assistant's accomplishments,* he grumbled and tripped over his skis for the millionth time. A swish of powder alerted him to Lucy's presence. Trying to keep up with the woman felt impossible, ironic really... She'd been trying to keep up with him for weeks.

"Jace, don't give up..." Now she called him Jace. Now, when he struggled like an infant just to remain upright. He forced his shoulders to relax and lifted his eyes to meet her hope-filled baby blues. A man could get lost in those angel eyes and pouty lips. Bring on the torture as long as she stuck by his side.

He determined to try again and nodded toward the lift. "Alright, let's try the instrument of torture again. I'll take this hill or die trying." He wiggled his eyebrows and shoved toward the lift. She giggled.

"The other way, he-man." He rolled his eyes and did his best to maneuver the skis the opposite direction. A moment later, the lift carried them both to the top of the mountain.

"So, Lucy... any instruction on how to get of this monstrosity?"

"Lift your skis, keep them straight, stand up and let the lift do the rest," she directed as they approached the pushing off point. *Skis up, skis straight, stand...*

Without warning, a skier fell in front of them. He swerved to miss the downed man, but before he could celebrate, his ski caught with another skier. He struggled to keep from crushing the poor victim. Raising up on one arm, he came nose to nose with his lovely assistant.

She raised a delicate brow. "Why, Mr. Sheridan!" She did the last thing he expected… lifting her head, she pressed her lips to his in one brief moment of heaven. Two seconds later, she shoved him off playfully and righted herself, leaving him stunned and tangled in the snow.

She laughed and threw a snowball at him before offering a hand up. He blinked. The flirtations of his personal assistant released something inside. He reached for her offered hand, and tugged her back into the snow beside him. Laughter rang out across the hillside. He tugged her close and returned her simple kiss in kind. Nothing passionate, just simple joy. Who is *this woman?* He marveled.

"Since I am in the presence of an expert skier, how do you suggest we untangle from this mess and get down the mountain. A Jublanovian cocoa and a warm fire with good company suddenly sounds inviting," he winked.

Lucy feigned disappointment. "You don't find the mountain top experience particularly inviting?" she teased with a rosy-lipped pout.

He tapped her rosy lips with a gloved finger. "The mountain top experience definitely invites more exploration, but perhaps a warm environment…" he rubbed his gloves together, "is the best plan." His traitorous teeth began to chatter. Lucy offered mercy, and demonstrated the best way to stand.

Back on his feet, he studied the beautiful mountain tops surrounding their position. *The Creator must have spent extra time here. The snow-*

capped mountains and tall pine forests are breathtakingly majestic.

Lucy made it to her feet beside him and followed his gaze with a deep breath and a smile. He studied her joy and thanked his Creator. The glorious creation beside him lightened his load and brightened his every moment. He could not imagine life without her.

I've got to find a way to keep her, God. Would you show me the way? Who is this amazing woman You dropped into my path?

Ask her.

The Voice echoed in his frozen brain. God's Voice… spoken to him… Lucy was speaking. He turned his attention her direction.

"Ready to head downhill? It's not too steep on this trail, but if you get going to fast form your skis into a wedge and press inward."

Twenty minutes and only one fall later, they arrived back at the lodge. The promise of a hot shower beckoned. Lucy waved him on.

"We have a private dining room reserved for dinner. I'll meet you there in an hour, boss."

He stopped dead in his tracks and turned. "No more 'boss', understand!" he insisted. "Jace, please, Lucy?" She nodded with an accepting smile. "Jace, I'll see you at dinner."

"How do I dress?"

"Nothing fancy. Jeans and a sweater will do. The resort is exclusive for friends of the royal family, a safe place to be yourself…" She saluted and glided down the hallway toward the elevator. "Your room is 405 by the way." She tossed him the key just before the elevator doors closed leaving him alone and wondering if Jacques completed the background check.

He desired this woman more than all the gold in his bank account. More than anything, he wanted to make her his wife. If only the report would show her eligible. He pulled out his phone and dialed the one person who could dash his hopes.

Jacque answered. "Yes, Mr. Sheridan."

Jace juggled the phone and tried his hotel key. The little light turned green on the door. He pushed down the handle to enter and nearly dropped the phone at the view from his room. A fire roared in a marble firepit in the center of a large sitting area with the entire mountain peak as a backdrop through a glass wall that ran the extent of the room.

"Wow... I mean, Jacque, any word on my assistant's background?"

Silence met him. "Jacque, are you still there?" He tossed the hotel key on a lamp table and lowered his battered form into the depths of the soft white sofa. The man on the other end cleared his throat.

"Master Sheridan, I am currently at liberty to tell you two things, but have been asked to keep detail for a further date. The first... Miss Lucy Christianson, your personal assistant *is* of the eligible house of the Christianson's of Jublanovia."

"Oh, praise God!" Jace exclaimed in relief and moved the phone to the other ear. "What's the second thing you are at liberty to share? She's not already spoken for... is she?" he demanded and waited with bated breath for the answer.

"The second item is that the Christianson family

requested a similar workup on you, Sir, and just received the king's approval. Pending your grandfather's approval, a match will be pursued by the Jublanovia house."

"I assume you contacted him… does Grandfather approve? He refused the last two."

"Your grandfather is delighted, Sir. Papers are being drawn up as we speak."

"Last question, Jacque. Does Lucy know?"

"I believe that is *your part* in this affair, Sir, not mine. I draw up marriage documents, but its up to *you* to woo the lady in question," his dry tone caused Jace to chuckle.

"Indeed, it is, good man. Thank you, Jacque."

"You're welcome, Sir. I wish you all the best."

After hanging up the call, Jace buried his head in his hand and soaked in the moment. His phone rang, showing the number of his VP of operations for Sheridan Energy. He answered. Half an hour later, a contract to buy out his company pinged his email.

Chapter Eight

Lucy finally dismissed the stylist who continued to fuss with her hair. The frustrated woman left the room leaving an equally frustrated Lucy in her wake. A massage and a hair stylist sent as a gift from the king's office disrupted rather than helped her peace of mind. She forced her thoughts to pleasant lines and wondered how to proceed.

A text from Krister stated that Jace was now informed of two things: her eligibility and her family's willingness to pursue a match. His grandfather and her cousin both agreed to a marriage, but what did Jace think? All marriage talk occurred quietly between the family heads in their respective lives, yet between the two of them? They'd barely begun to use first names. How did they move forward?

She slipped into her fitted jeans and a soft, white Angora sweater. A knock sounded on the door to her suite. A maid answered and returned with four dozen crimson roses. She pulled the card out of its envelope before releasing the maid to find a vase.

> To my unexpected assistant,
> My help, My delight,
> Four dozen roses for each of the short weeks we've shared…
> Would you consider a sharing a lifetime with me?
> Let's talk.
> Jace

Lucy paled. Could she, a member of the royal family actually obtain a love match? Jace, with his brilliant mind, and insane work pace captured her heart and made her feel needed, but did he care? How could she know?

The phone rang. She glanced at the number… her cousin, King David. Two weeks ago, he'd endured the loss of his unborn child, making her once again, his heir apparent. In his grief, her laid back relative pushed her to find a match. Jace Sheridan's background worked, but how did Jace feel?

Their time on the mountain rang through her memory. Hesitating to answer what she knew would be excitement or pressure, she pushed accept on the phone and answered anyway. One didn't ghost the king.

David spoke with calm authority on the other end. "Lucinda… How are you?" He inquired.

Taking a deep breath, she forced the truth to her lips. "Pressured, uncertain, and though I know both families are excited, I have no idea how the man in question feels about the idea. It's *never* even come up! I've acted as the man's personal assistant!"

A deep chuckled echoed. "I *still* can't believe you hired on as someone's personal assistant, Luce! What were you thinking? You've been trained to run a county, not someone's errands. How does it feel to be on the receiving end of giving commands?"

Lucy took a second to reflect. "Honestly…? He's brilliant, passionate, disorganized and cares little for the everyday details, but he's a caring individual… a great boss, but as a spouse or soulmate… we've only known each other for a few weeks! We've never even hinted to one another about a relationship until yesterday. He doesn't know at the moment that I'm heir to the throne!"

Sadness reflected in the heaviness of David's sigh. "I'm sorry this is your burden, Lucy. I truly understand. Silvia and I were given a deadline to marry in three weeks, remember? I praise God for the love match He blessed me with in that woman. Is there any chance for such a love with you and Mr. Sheridan? I don't wish to force an unwanted union although you know the position I'm in. I pray there are more children in our future, but…"

Lucy cut him short. "I understand, David. We're family. The burden of the crown rests on us both. Feelings are growing; we just haven't spoken. However, just before you called, I received the most romantic bouquet of roses and a note hinting about a future. Jace wants to talk. I'm just at a loss how to move forward," she confessed with a sigh.

"That's wonderful, Luce…! Just let him take the lead, okay? I know you have the higher rank in the country, but in a marriage partnership, he should take the lead. Silvia runs a billion-dollar cocoa conglomerate and is my right arm in the kingdom, but we are in it together in marriage. She supports me, holds my feet to the fire, loves me, reminds me of the truth in God's word. Does this man know our Lord, Lucy?"

"That's just it, David, we haven't spoken about it. I did see him pray over lunch once."

"Talk to him, Lucinda. Give me an answer two days before the ball. I'll stall his people until then. Deal?"

"In this instance, my king, I am grateful for your leadership. Had it been your father or brother…" she paused not wanting to say how rigid and hardline both men would have been. She had not wished to speak ill of those who'd gone before.

"Thank you, Lucy. Say no more. I never wanted to be king, yet here I am serving in the name of our Lord. I pray every day for wisdom from the King of all Kings. Silvia and I are praying for you and Mr. Sheridan. Let me know your answer."

"I will your Majesty, my king."

"Luce…"

"It's appropriate in the moment, King David. Please receive it as a sign of my utmost respect for your wisdom and leadership. Blessings to both you and Silvia from our Lord and Savior, Jesus Christ. You will have my answer soon."

He disconnected the phone just as a knock sounded on her door. A lady's maid provided by the king answered the door revealing her attractive boss and *future husband if things continue to progress,* she mused.

He cleared his throat and with hands clasp behind his back gave a slight nod. "Might I come in, Lucy? He queried. His eyes fell on the roses, and he raised one dark eyebrow. "I see you got my message." He stepped into the sitting area when she nodded her consent.

"May I have your reply…? It appears our families are in communication. I would like to discuss the merger with you alone, if you are not opposed." He spoke in veiled terms since they were not alone.

Lucy nodded and dismissed the maid. The moment the young woman stepped out of the room, he came to her and took her manicured hands in his own strong ones. "Lucy, I wasn't looking," he started. "I'd given up hope quite honestly. Then you came into my life and I found hope for the first time in a long time."

His dark eyes searched hers. "I know our families seek a match between us. You been an amazing assistant… and I would *love* to hear why in the world someone with your status took the job… but I'm interested in knowing if you can see me as something more? I am definitely interested if it helps…"

A million feelings and considerations flooded her normally organized brain. Taking a moment to form her answer, she dropped to the plush sofa and patted the seat next to her.

Jace studied her with cautious eyes.

"May I ask a couple of personal questions?"

He nodded, so she plunged forward.

"What is your personal faith or religious belief?"

Leaning forward, he rested his forearms on his knees and clasp his hands. "Ah, important question. Let's see… I'm a risk taker, action maker guy, but I belief in the higher authority of Almighty God, Maker of heaven and earth. I believe all humans have sinned and fallen short of the glory of God, but that Jesus Christ, God in the flesh, paid the penalty for that sin and offers salvation as a free gift. I received that gift as a young man of fourteen. I need to get better at walking with him daily though, and I need to be involved in a local church. And what do you believe, Lucy?" He countered.

Relief coursed through her veins. She offered a genuine smile that started at her heart and pushed outward to her lips. "The same. Oh, Jace, I'm *so* glad to hear you confess Christ."

His lips curled in a masculine, confident grin. He leaned back and crossed his arms. "Why, Lucy? Why are you happy to hear of my faith?" he pressed.

With a shy, demure glance she whispered, "Because I've… come to care for you and could never consider a future unless…"

"…I too professed Christ," he finished. She nodded. "What else?" he prodded.

"Children…?" She bit her lip to ask the awkward question.

He threw his head back and laughed rubbing his chin. "I believe *that* is the whole point of this crazy arrangement between our families, correct? That the *line* may continue… That said, I'd like at least four.

Being an only child is no fun. How about you?"

She felt the blood rush to her cheeks. "The same."

"Then back to the original question... would you consider a lifetime by my side in marriage?"

She hesitated, bit her lip and studied his earnest face complete with five o'clock shadow. "There is one other very important consideration. I know you are in line as heir to..."

He waved her off. "I'm fifth in line to a throne which no-longer holds power, Lucy. If that's what worries you..." She held up her hand and shook her head.

"It's not *your* family which is the concern. It's mine. I'm currently the principle heir to the actual Jublanovian throne... the "Crown Princess" if you will."

His eyes widened and he opened and closed his mouth then spoke. "But I thought... King David and Queen Silvia... you are his first cousin?"

She nodded and let him process.

"I read that his father and elder brother died. Your father passed away as well..." Again, she nodded.

He raised his dark eyes to meet hers. "But the king and queen recently announced they were expecting a child..." It was more a question than a statement.

Lucy sighed. "For a few brief months, the pressure left me. Two weeks ago, while attending a hockey match, the crowds went wild. Caught in the crush, Queen Silvia suffered a severe blow to her abdomen and spine. She lost the baby, and only

David, the doctor and I know that she may or may not be able to carry another child. Her body guards saved her, but right now… they are heartbroken. David is pressuring me to secure the throne. I… wanted you to know. Jublanovia and I are a package deal. Perhaps, Queen Silvia will recover. If she does not, it is up to me to provide an heir…"

She cast her eyes down to the floor in embarrassment. *Who speaks this way anymore?* Her heart didn't know its own mind. The feelings for Jace were so new.

He rubbed his jaw and grinned. "And I thought my obligations provided challenges. Wow," Suddenly, he winked. "The future queen wants me to father her children…? Quite the topic for the first date, Lucy," he teased. "You are a rather unexpected assistant. Still, the question remains… why me? Do you want me? Queen or personal assistant, I cannot imagine life without you by my side. Don't answer me now. I have a lovely dinner planned. Afterward, I thought a sleighride or ice-skating would be romantic and isolated. Your choice."

He held out a hand and stood. "Join me?"

Pleased at the change of topic, she accepted the hand, and sent a thank you heavenward. She needed time.

Chapter Nine

Jace paced his room. Dinner by a massive stone fireplace alone with Lucinda Christianson felt like home. Bringing him to Jublanovia cost Lucy. The burdens of the crown fell heavy on her shoulders the moment their surprising ski adventure ended and wedding conversations began.

God, help me to know and understand her needs. As my personal assistant, she reordered my world and brought peace. Show me how to do the same for her.

Seek me.

Jace opened his Bible for the first time in months and began to read. Peace came. He checked his watch. Lucy hesitantly chose ice-skating for their date. He shook his head in confusion. The occasional glimpse he caught of the woman beneath the organization and confidence fascinated him. Her love of speed, sports cars, tiaras, and skiing hinted of passion, yet the moment they stepped into discussion of marriage and her Jublanovian duty to the crown that woman vanished.

He stepped toward the French doors leading to a lovely balcony overlooking the snow-capped mountains and breathed deeply of the fresh air. His head cleared and his mind recalled the Scripture reading from moments before: "If you believe, you will receive whatever you ask for in prayer."

The urge to pray for the woman God created grew as did the desire to bring joy and romance into her life. He stared at the mountain and remember Christ and his promise of power.

God, you brought my perfect match to be this billionaire's unexpected assistant. I bring the concept of marriage with Lucy to you. Show us how… show me how may I use the power and resources you've entrusted to me for your purpose and glory.

The desire to spoil his Lucy, his unexpected assistant, welled up within him unlike any previous feelings for a woman in his life. The others wanted something from him. Lucy only gave and asked nothing in return. His attempt at alleviating the seriousness failed miserably. Suggesting she needed him to father her children forced Lucy into a retreat.

How can I show her she matters?

Inspiration struck. He called the rink, rented the entire place for the evening and paid all the vendors double their normal intake to leave a gourmet cocoa and dessert basket. The need to show his romantic side pushed him to order a horse-drawn sleigh to drive them to the outdoor rink. A call to the local furrier delivered several furs, hats and gloves to Lucy's suite for her careful selection.

An hour and several details later, Jace waited

confidently in the carriage. Ten minutes passed, twenty, thirty… Lucy always showed up on time. Concerned, he paid the driver and sent him away before running the four floors to Lucy's suite and wondering with each step if he misread her heart.

No one answered, yet it opened the moment he touched the door. He entered, but stopped in surprise just inside. Lucy sat among the furs, crying her eyes out. He slipped down beside her and offered his handkerchief, grateful for once that the habit drilled into him by his grandfather came in handy.

She snatched it up and blew her nose in a very uncharacteristic trumpet. He hid a smile. "What's the matter, dearest Lucy? Surely its not all that terrible. Say the word, and I'll fix it."

Brightly colored toes poked out from under the soft beaver fur while her normally pristine blond hair stuck out of a messy bun. Adorable came to mind. She blew her nose and shook her head as the waterworks started again.

"You can't help," she moaned. "No one can. I don't know what to feel right now."

He brushed her hair aside and rubbed her aching neck. Leaning into his touch, she sniffed, then blinked.

"Oh no! I ruined our date… Oh Jace, I'm so sorry! It just that His Majesty the King called and…" The tears threatened to flow again, but she shoved them aside and took a deep breath. "I'm devastated for Silvia. The specialist just spoke with them. She'll make a full recovery, but they say it's likely she'll never have another child."

She paused and scooted around to face him, her face a mixture of grief and frustration. "King David just called an emergency meeting of the council. Since my father's death, I hold a seat. I'm to get to the palace as soon as possible."

Jace rose to his feet. *This* he could help with in a tangible way. "Done. I'll call the pilot. It's only a thirty-minute flight. After the meeting, I'll take you somewhere special… anywhere you like, Lucy." He reached for her hands and pulled her to her feet and into his embrace.

She buried her head in his chest and wept. "That won't be possible, Jace. My king ordered me to the meeting and gave me a heads up to his announcement. He's going to step aside and back into his former role as Finance Minister to the Throne since he can no longer fully assume the duties of king. He's insisting I assume the throne in his place."

Jace pulled back and roared. "That's ludicrous! The man can remain king for his entire lifetime. Upon his death, the closest relative would step up. Why step aside now?" he demanded.

Lucy placed a finger on his lips.

"David and Silvia are devasted right now. They aren't thinking correctly, but he *is* the king, and I must bow to his demands. I told him I would consider a temporary provision as Silvia recovers, but in reality, I have no choice if he insists."

She wiped her tears and straightened. "At least I had a few months of freedom. I truly enjoyed being your assistant," she whispered.

He hugged her close and answered softly in her

ear. "Why did you do it, Lucinda Danae Christianson? Why assist me when you were born to power, money and leadership?"

She sniffed and offered a smile. "Everyone needs help, Jace. I understand. Leadership doesn't happen in a vacuum. A leader needs qualified people surrounding him or her. I know how to run a kingdom which is essentially what you have. I possessed the skills you needed, had the time and... God told me to help bring peace to your world. Now... I'm called to bring peace to my family and my trouble little kingdom.

Jublanovia has endured much sorrow in the last three to four years. The people need a time of peace and security. David knows this. Silvia knows this. I know this. Will you come with me? I'm allowed to bring only one assistant into the meeting. Security is high right now, but since you are a member of a royal house, and have been vetted already by the king, there shouldn't be a problem."

Jace rubbed the back of his neck and tried to slow his whirling mind at the turn of events. Lucy focused on the moment, on her cousin's grief, on the council meeting and the weight of the crown, but he knew how the meeting would play out if he went. In the past four years, the kingdom suffered the loss of it's primary king, its crown prince, and now the second son crowned king was unable to produce an heir.

Lucy would not only be forced to take the throne, but it would be contingent upon their immediate marriage. King David was forcing Jace's hand, and they both knew it. Only Lucy appeared blind to that detail.

The lady in question blinked up at him with hope in her eyes. He decided to keep the moment light until he could fully commit to the new turn of events.

"Of course, I'll attend, but..." he chuckled. "Who is the unexpected assistant now?" he teased. "I see how you've turned the tables... but I guarantee you are a much greater help in your role as assistant than I will be in mine. You've seen how I drop details."

She grinned. "Only when you're bored. When you put your mind to it..." she snuggled his fur gift to her chest. "I'm *really sorry* I missed this date. Care to escort the Crown Princess to a meeting instead of a romantic sleighride and a starlit evening ice-skating?"

He bent and kissed her nose. "Your wish is my command, Your Royal Highness, Ma'am."

He left her with the lady's maid and hurried to command the airplane, cancel the evening plans, and take care of the furrier bill. A quick call delivered the cocoa and goodie basket to the plane. His phone rang. The number on the screen lit with the buyer for his company. Ghosting the man no longer seemed the best option. He quickly took the call and set up a conference call with the principles of his business to be handled during the flight.

Unlocking the door to his suite, he paused to take in the beautiful view and settle in front of the fire. Lucy's maid rang with the message her Royal Highness would be awaiting the limo in half an hour. The fire pleasantly crackled as snow began to fall outside the glass wall. The moment beckoned for reflection.

For almost a month, Lucy Christianson moved through every waking moment of his life. First, as the amazing assistant answering to his every whim, beck and call. Now, with roles reversed, he desperately needed this moment to take stock of what he really desired. Where did his calling rest?

A butler delivered a latte and a message on a silver platter. Grateful for the one and curious for the other, he took a sip and savored the nutty flavor as he opened the envelop marked simply... JACE.

My dear Jace,

It just occurred to me, as I'm certain it already has to you with that fast brain of yours, just what I asked of you. The council will be expecting an immediate announcement from me. I'm certain the king thinks it is a formality given the arrangements being made on our behalf, but you and I never settled this match between us. Certainly, not with the stringent demands now in play.

I appreciate the use of your jet, but please.... You are free to live without these bonds I come with. I am a package deal."

Come on, Lucy... just ask me. He needed her to say the words, needed her to want him. If she asked, he would marry her tonight and give her the children the kingdom so desperately desired. He'd spend a lifetime assisting her service to the kingdom, providing for and spoiling her at every possible opportunity. The woman selflessly gave to everyone around her.

Ask me, Lucy... He resolved in strength to

propose, but in heart… he wanted her to ask. His eyes continued reading.

"Jace, I'm trying desperately to set you free, but I need you by my side."

That's my girl! His heart soared and pounded in his chest. He kept reading.

"You asked me before all this mess, if I could love or want you. I already do. The moment you asked me to take care of you in that old convenience store, I wanted the job. Now, it seems I need to ask you the same question. I'm being called to take care of a kingdom, but I can't do it alone.

The highest role I could offer you would be Prince of the Realm… crazy since that now makes you the 'assistant' like you joked. If I accept your original proposal, would you accept mine? If King David keeps the throne, I desire to stay by your side as your wife, assisting you in any project or venture you desire. If he steps down, and I assume the throne would you be threatened if I asked you to stand by my side? Either way, I'd like to accept your proposal and be your wife.

I treasure the crazy, brief time we've shared and await your answer on the plane."

Very Sincerely Yours,
HRH Princess Lucinda Danae Christianson
Your,
Lucy

Jace downed the rest of the latte, and jumped to his feet. His Lucy needed him, wanted him. He called the butler and ordered a bouquet filled with seven varieties of flowers… any flowers just as long as there were seven varieties. He crafted the note to follow the Scandinavian tradition, instructing Lucy to place the seven varieties under her pillow so she might dream of her true love.

A second phone call, ordered the jewelry shop in the lodge to deliver three of their most expensive diamond rings.

"I'll pay for all three in a size six, just send me one traditional engagement ring fit for a queen, one marquise diamond, and one emerald cut surrounded by rubies or sapphires if you have it. It must be at my room in the next twenty minutes or the deal is off."

The man stammered his surprise and quickly agreed.

Jace plopped down again, exhausted from the emotional rollercoaster, and with a call to the front desk to wake him in fifteen minutes, promptly fell asleep.

Chapter Ten

King David Christianson solemnly grasped Jace's hand. With sorrowful eyes, the man studied him. Jace knew what he asked. Stepping up would not be a problem, yet he couldn't help but see the wisdom in the eyes of the man before him.

"Walk with me…" the King commanded and waved off his attendants. Jace followed him through the columned marble hallway, passed guards and servants to the outside balcony. Once outside, the man shut the heavy doors behind him and turned to Jace.

"You know what I'm asking?"

Jace nodded, uncertain how much leeway his position allowed.

"What are your thoughts, Mr. Sheridan? I need honesty. How is Lucy?"

Christmas lights bejeweled the palace grounds creating a festive atmosphere. The kingdom knew nothing of the sorrow.

"May I speak honestly, Your Majesty?"

King David gave him a weary nod. "And

please… in private, call me David. You are a member of a royal house and almost family I am hoping. I could use a moment of honest conference. Is Lucy alright? I fear I am overburdening you both at the beginning of your relationship, but its no less of a burden than I bear."

"Your Majesty… David, Lucy is able to bear the load, and I plan to stand by her side, but perhaps I may offer a bit of perspective…" When the king nodded, he continued. "In recent years, your country has suffered great loss. Switching monarchs now will stir dissention and uncertainty.

Your council could appoint Lucy the heir apparent, and quietly, as you and your wife recuperate, she and they could carry the load for a few months. You retain the crown, Lucy bears your burden for a time but regains her freedom, and the kingdom retains its stability. Who knows but that once healed, your wife may conceive and bear another child?"

"The doctors don't think…" Tears formed as the king began.

Jace lay a hand on his shoulder. "Doctors have been wrong before. If our Heavenly Father speaks the word, I learning we are to walk faith and not doubt… Didn't Christ say something along the lines that if we believe, we will receive whatever we ask for in prayer. What is God telling you in this moment, Your Majesty… I mean… David?"

The man met his eyes, startled by the question. "This morning, before the diagnosis, He gave me that very verse about receiving whatever I ask in prayer… which I promptly forgot when the doctors gave their report. I think I expected the report to be the answer, yet God the Father knew the report and gave that promise to me ahead of time!" He wiped his eyes and shook Jace's hand.

"Thank you, brother. I rarely get the opportunity to speak with anyone freely. Normally, my wife fills that role, but she could not this time. Thank you for the reminder of truth." He straightened. "I will have the council name Lucy as my successor *until* another child is born. If Lucy would quietly lead the council in my stead while I comfort my wife for a season, I will stay on until God says otherwise."

He paused and cocked his head. "I have one request, if it is to your liking…"

Jace spread his hands. "How may I assist you?"

"May we still announce a royal wedding at the Christmas ball? And if so, might it be in the spring so my Silvia may assist in planning it? Helping Lucy with the wedding, especially creating wedding delicacies, will restore her joy and purpose. She just got on her feet and is already stress baking and inventing new cocoas. It's her therapy… and my burden," he chuckled with a pat to his stomach. I'm constantly in the gym already!"

Jace threw his head back and laughed. "I heard you married a cocoa heiress! Such a heavy burden… a wife that stress bakes! The answer is a definite yes to all of the above. Anything I should know about how Lucy destresses?"

King David's eyes twinkled. "She likes to go fast. Cars… you should see her collection! She flies planes and adores skiing! Silvia might be a danger to my middle, but Lucy…? For such a composed, gracious lady, she is a bit of an adrenaline junkie. It's her way of release against all the duty and obligation, I guess."

Jace nodded. "And yours…?"

The king smiled. "Horses. I love the freedom and affection they offer. Shall we go in? My keepers will be pacing. With the exception of Lucy, the council is unaware of why they have been called. Now… I will have three announcements. Your wedding announcement provides a happy distraction. I will announce the loss of our child and the need for Lucy to be named heir apparent once again."

They stepped into the palace and faced the assembled group. Lucy appeared at his side. He smiled down at her and whispered. "We are the happy announcement. Be prepared. The king and I have come to an agreement."

Her eyes widened in surprise before settling in a smile.

"Miracle working assistant…" she teased. "What other details did you work out?"

"That we will be married in spring, that the queen will help plan the menu for the wedding. That…"

"Did you say the 'queen'?"

"Yep. Unexpected? Am I the best assistant you ever had, your Royal Highness?"

She elbowed him secretly and turned her brightest smile his direction. "You are a very unexpected assistant, sir. I believe I'll keep you, or will you keep me, perhaps?"

"I propose a life long partnership, my love,

always by each other's side. Agreed?"

"Agreed." She whispered.

His phone buzzed on silent. Glancing at the number, he paled. "I must take this…" With a nod at the king, he hurried out of the room.

"Jacque, you used the family emergency code. What is it?"

The faithful family servant spoke in a solemn tone he rarely used. Concern filled Jace's heart. "There are three items requiring attention, Sir. The first, your grandfather is ill, and just requested your presence. The second, the home country…, just did the unthinkable and announced its intention to reinstate the monarchy."

Jace paced the Christmas lit gardens aware of the big announcement Lucy faced alone. "What? When has that ever happened? Well, Uncle Karl must be ecstatic. I will leave in the morning to see Grandfather, but while this is incredible news, Jacque, my wedding announcement is being made to the Jublanovian council, and Lucy has just been announced the heir apparent. Is there something else? I need to get inside."

The announcement met with silence. "We might have a problem, Sir."

Jace tapped his foot on the cold marble in impatience. "Spit it out, Jacque. I must go."

"Very well, I will *spit it out* as it were. Your grandfather somehow convinced our country to bring back the monarchy by informing them of your alliance with Jublanovia. He just bypassed the four other heir in line for the throne and named you the next king of Lichtnovia."

Silence. Jace dropped to a conveniently, placed garden bench afraid his knees might give way.

"Jacques, our family has been banished from setting foot in Lichtnovia for decades. There is no kingdom. Lichtnovia is a democracy now. It has been since Grandfather was seventeen years old. Our lands were confiscated. Even if the family lands and crown were reinstated... I'm what? Fifth in line. I'm the youngest grandchild of the youngest sibling who is a female... no less. I'm the last in line!"

The voice on the other end grew silent and then the voice of his grandfather echoed through the phone. The man *never* used technology. "Jacian! You are the only one of my family worth anything! The only one to care about an old man's dreams, to actually invest in and manage the family history, portfolios and investments, as well as the only one to truly marry an eligible royal mate. The others married wealth but not royalty. My choice is clear. You have five days to clear and coordinate your affairs.

Our people want their monarchy back. You must return and make the royal wedding announcement at the Lichtnovia palace on Christmas Eve. Invitations just went out to all the royal houses of Europe to attend a coronation ball. The wedding may take place in Jublanovia, but the announcement and coronation will need to be attended in our country. Congratulations, your Majesty," he chuckled. The phone call ended.

Jace stood unable to move and then burst out laughing. The Christmas lights alone heard his folly. In an unbelievable turn of events, he now held the higher office once again. King…? What was this crazy game of life they led? What would happen if King David and Queen Silvia could not conceive? Would they reign over both nations? Reign…? He could barely stay in one place for two days? Emotions so thick he couldn't decipher them swirled. He shook his head, knelt and humbly cried out for wisdom from Almighty God.

His head cleared. At the moment, Lucy needed him. His feet carried him back into the royal Jublanovian hall just as the King announced the loss of his unborn child and Lucy's renewed status as heir apparent.

The council reeled in shock. Lucy's eyes glistened with tears. The great mahogany table bore the burdens of many as: heads rested, fists pounded, and eyes studied the ancient glossy surface. He studied the room with the eyes of a king. He'd been right to tell King David to retain power. These people didn't need to lose both the infant hope and their king and queen.

He glanced at the king, who nodded. Five minutes ago, the announcement seemed so simple. Now… should he announce just the marriage or his coronation or both? He needed kingly counsel. He bent to whisper in Lucy's ear. He and Lucy needed one another to keep from being tossed to and fro by the storms of life.

"I need a short recess to bend the king's ear. Is there a precedent you can call? It's a royal emergency." Concern lit a fire in her eyes. She stepped forward in her role as head of the council.

"The Council will come to order." The room quieted. "Our condolences to the King and Queen in this time of deep loss," her gentle voice cracked. "I'm sure we all agree to give them time at the country palace to rest and recover, so that they may be blessed by Christ our King with a new life in the future. King David, know that for the next three months, the council will do it's best to unburden you as much as possible." The King nodded his genuine thanks. She proceeded.

"Now, we have an exciting announcement to make, but would like to take a thirty-minute recess out of respect for our King. The palace staff is here to serve your needs and is offering a light pastry and cocoa or coffee thanks to the thoughtfulness of our still recovering queen. Nods of approval and condolences milled about the room, as Lucy followed him with a nod to the king.

Once out of the room, she directed him to a small, alcove almost invisible due to the large tapestry covering the wall.

"I intercepted the king. He will be here the moment he can slip away. What is it, Jace? I saw you run out."

He rubbed the back of his neck and shook his head as he pulled her next to him on a brocaded loveseat. By the time he explained the turn of events, the king ducked into the tiny room. Once again, he explained the fantastic turn of events. Instead of frustration, the king grinned and slapped his back. Lucy sat stunned.

"So... five minutes after you remind me to walk in truth and stay faithful, you receive the call that

Lucy is not only heir apparent to Jublanovia, making you a Prince of the Realm, but now you are King of our sister country, and you plan to make her your queen? Who's assisting who anymore?" He chuckled. "Partners for life, how fabulous. So how do you want us to play this with the council?"

Jace explained his grandfather's orders. King David nodded his approval. Both royal houses get a celebration. I concur. Now... before we go back to make our announcement, may we call Queen Silvia and give her the news. Lucy, request her help, her advice, anything to bring hope right now."

A phone call and an announcement later, Jace and Lucy took a deep breath under the canopy of lights and stars. As partners, they held hands and walked through the colorful winter gardens lit for Christmas.

Chapter Eleven:

<u>Five months later...</u>

Lucy sat with Queen Silvia in the royal Jublanovian spring gardens and took a moment to breathe between events. The Queen giggled. "A week of coronation balls in one country and now a royal wedding and with endless balls in another. I adore your ice blue and silver theme, but wherever did you have the time to hunt up so many ice blue ball gowns? Laughter bubbled up bringing refreshment.

"Most are from an amazing little shop in Geneva. My "boss" paid for it all. Jace definitely flexed his billionaire muscles that day... never knowing about the closet full of dresses at home." She shrugged. "He said he wanted someone to spend money on... so I let him," she said with a mischievous grin.

"Of course, the wedding gown is from the designers in my country." Lucy placed a gentle hand on the soft round mound of her cousin-in-law's belly. "How is our youngest citizen today? Are you both okay?"

The Queen's smile dimmed at the corners. "Baby is fine, and I am grateful. I miss the one I never met, but I am blessed by this little miraculous life. David will hardly let me out of his sight. Attending your wedding and the ball afterward is the highlight of my confinement. He's only allowing me to visit small, closely monitored groups until this little one is born. I'm rather okay with his protectiveness for now."

A tall shadow fell across their laps as her cousin, King David approached with a nod at Lucy and a tender kiss for his wife. "Ladies, it's time to prepare. The wedding begins shortly, and I've been sent to fetch the bride."

Two hours later, lilies of the valley, blue iris, white peony, blue hydrangea, baby's breath, white roses and blue bells graced her bouquet. Seven flowers for the man of her dreams. Her motorcycle riding, reckless boss, her billionaire, her Prince of the Realm, her King awaited her at the altar of the Jublanovian Church of Our Savior in his royal uniform complete with a long black morning coat, striped trousers and silver noble vest and four-in-hand tie. An ice blue sash completed the dashing look of Lichtnovia's new King.

The grand pipe organ pealed out magnificent notes. She squeezed her cousin's arm. King David, resplendent in his royal blue and red uniform nodded and tapped her hand. Slowly, the two proceeded down the long, red carpeted aisle to the music. Upon reaching the steps of dais, the waiting minister addressed the Jublanovian king.

"Who gives this woman to this man in holy matrimony?" he queried.

"I do." King David's royal voice rang out. The king of Jublanovia awarded her hand to the new king of Lichtnovia. Jace's rugged face lit with joy. He winked as their hands touched, igniting the fire of passion in her soul. Before Christ and kingdom, they pledged their loyalty, faithfulness and love. Two hearts entwined as one.

Finally, the minister pronounced them husband and wife.

"King Jacian Augustus Habsperg Sheridan... you may kiss your Queen."

Her Jace pressed his lips tenderly to her own and escorted her to the balcony outside. As the doors opened to greet the public, he leaned in close and whispered.

"You, Lucinda Danae Christianson Habsperg-Sheridan are the greatest, most unexpected gift of my life: greater than a billion-dollar fortune, greater than a kingdom, I have only question to ask in this first moment of our grand partnership of life..."

She gazed up into his smiling face in wonder. "Anything for you, Jace. What is it?"

"Want to go speedboat racing in the Mediterranean for a honeymoon?"

The crowd roared with laughter as their new King realized his question rang out through the nest of microphones buried in the ice blue and white flowers. He laughed good naturedly and cleared his throat.

"Just testing to see if the microphones are working..." he grinned with a wink at Lucy's red face. He kissed her cheek and whispered. "I have a plan B on standby." When the moment of waving passed, he dipped his queen and pressed a kiss to her lips for all the world to see.

Stephanie Guerrero is author of the novel Shades of the Orient and a number of novellas specializing in adventure romance!

When not writing, she enjoys: hiking, travel, exploring, research and all things chocolate. Christ is her inspiration in all things. Her husband and four children make "living the adventure" a joy.

She loves to hear from readers and can be found on Facebook as Stephanie Guerrero (author) or through email at warriorranch@yahoo.com .It's a good thing she loves hats, because she wears so many! She is enthusiastic in sharing that "happily ever after" isn't found just in fiction, but can be found when following God with all your heart!

Made in the USA
Columbia, SC
21 November 2019